WHISPER: THE PETE ZENDEL SERIES

A FULL LENGTH PREQUEL

JOY OHAGWU

LIFE FOUNTAIN BOOKS

INTRODUCTION

WHISPER- The PETE ZENDEL Christian Romantic
Suspense Series-

~

A Full Length Prequel

To JESUS- The One Who laughs. Your Holy Name is my Crown of Glory.

A CONTEMPORARY CHRISTIAN ROMANTIC SUSPENSE SERIES

Get Joy Ohagwu's starter Library for **FREE**. Details are at the end of this book.

Foundational Scripture

∾

"I am the Way, and the Truth, and the Life: no one comes to the Father but through Me."-**JESUS** (John 14:6)

1

"Then you shall know that I am in the midst of Israel: I am the Lord your God and there is no other. My people shall never be put to shame."- Joel 2:27

"911. What's your emergency?"

Rita Gonzalez gripped the phone tighter, covered her mouth with the other hand, and squatted low in a corner of the small, smoke-shrouded room. If she had still been in the outer office fixing appointments where the fire began, she feared she would've been history. But she'd gone to the file room to replace the client files they'd used earlier today, fix the notes taped to each file, and lock the cabinet drawers.

She came out only to see a fire raging from the reception

area. The gasoline smell stung her nostrils as the fire spread, and the heat tingled her skin. So she yanked the fire alarm. Then the explosion thudded in her ears. She dove into this file storage room and shut the door just before a second explosion rocketed through the building. She'd clasped her hands over her ears then felt her cellphone bulging out of her pants' pocket. She pulled it out and dialed 911.

Hungry flames licked the edges of the doorjamb, and the fire threatened to burst into the room, teasing her with yellow flashes underneath the door.

Any moment now, the fire will breach the last barrier—the door. "There's a fire. Please help me." A cough interrupted her and she doubled over. "It's almost inside here. The office is burning." Another bout of coughing halted her speech, and she flattened her palm on the brown carpet and bent over, inhaling a deep breath.

"You're going to be fine, honey. Find a place in the room away from the fire and get as close as you can to the ground. Use any clothing to cover your nose and mouth. If there is water around you, wet the cloth when you place it on your nose. Are you hurt? Are you alone?"

"Yes, I am alone."

"What's your address?"

She managed to call out the address before more smoke seeped in and white, smoky clouds blurred her view of the door. Fire crackled underneath the door, making her squirm. She was clearly trapped. "Please hurry."

"Help is on the way. I'll stay on the phone."

The operator kept speaking with her, but Rita scarcely heard her over the one question vibrating through her head: would the firefighters make it in time?

A spark shot farther from beneath the door. That drove her deeper and closer to the second-story window. She huddled near the glass, but when she glanced outside, she couldn't imagine going down so far. She could fracture a bone, so she refused to take the risk to jump.

The door burst open, and burning heat slammed her skin. She screamed, and the phone dropped from her hand, sliding closer to the flames.

A figure appeared out of the fire. But as he held out a hand to her, something about him made her pause. Clad in all black, he didn't have a county firefighter badge on his chest.

He wasn't a firefighter. She withdrew her hand, even though she was now finding it tough to breathe.

At her hesitation, he came closer. He bent over and caused her to shrink farther away as her heart pounded. "There wasn't supposed to be anyone in here." He crouched low and tipped her chin, forcing her to look up. "Now I have to take care of you too. Come here."

She pushed his hand back. "No!" Smoke stinging her eyes, she teared up. Yet she fought back.

He pulled her by her hair and forced her up to a standing

position. He showed her a printed photo, but she didn't look. "Where can I find this? I need the information."

"What?" She didn't look. "I don't know what you are talking about. Please leave me alone."

He yanked her arm and drew nearer to the fire burning the entrance. "Where are the files?"

"What files?" Had she heard a loud bang before going in the back to organize the file room? She was getting confused about what she heard and didn't hear. "Please let me go. I don't know anything."

The clog in her throat blocked even the smoky air, and gasping for breath, Rita started crying.

Another figure appeared beside him. "Let's go. It's not her we want. It's her boss. She's just the secretary. Hurry up. People are coming."

Voices calling out for any survivors reached her ears from afar, and Rita screamed with all the air left in her lungs. A slap hit her cheek and left it tingling and slammed her face to the ground. Then the man cursed. He shoved her to the corner, punched her face, and just before she blacked out, and the firefighters—the real firefighters entered—he left through the window. The accomplice followed. She was gasping for breath, and cough spasms wracked her body when a man rushed for her.

Caring arms lifted her and carried her out. "You are going to be fine. Hang on." Sure that she was now safe, she let her eyes slide shut.

"Hey, come and listen to this," Tatiana Stone, 911 operator, called to her supervisor. "Our last caller dropped her phone at some point, but I heard someone else there when she'd said she was alone. I think I also heard her scream. Maybe the fire wasn't an accident?"

She waited for her supervisor to listen to the recording. Then he nodded. "You might be right. I heard something. Send that to the police and let them handle it from there." He patted her shoulder. "Good job."

She picked up the phone and called the SSPD.

Miranda Sow listened to soft music as she flicked on her blinker and made the same set of turns down the valley as she'd made every Friday evening for two years, heading toward her office building. She turned off her AC and rolled her window down.

Then the burning smell hit her nostrils. As she drew closer and peered in the distance, her eyeballs rounded. She blinked, then gasped. From afar off, she saw fire department trucks had surrounded her building.

Huge flames flicked upward, and her hands tightened on the steering wheel. Wasn't that her office—on *fire*? Her chest constricted. She stepped up on the gas pedal, and just then, a car struck hers from behind. She gripped the wheel and righted the vehicle. Then she rounded the second to the last set of hills and slowed down, catching a glimpse of the dark Tundra behind her. Why did he hit her? If this wasn't an unsafe place to stop to prevent an accident, she would stop now. But she moved forward toward a wider section of the road.

"Maybe he's new around here." The car neared at a higher-than-average speed, and instead of passing like she expected, it slammed her rear bumper again, harder this time.

Her heart pounded in her chest, and she scrambled with her other hand for her phone. This wasn't an accident. This person meant her harm. If she could find her phone with one hand, hidden inside her purse, under her last patient's files, she might just...

Her fingers fumbled fast. A third ram sent her car into a double spin across the road. Losing control, she pumped her brakes to prevent it from skidding off the valley, but the wheels wouldn't grip the asphalt. Off it plunged into the grove of trees and tumbled down the valley. Her head hit the steering wheel twice, and her own voice screaming provided the last sounds she heard before the car burst into flames.

2

"*THEN THE REMNANT OF JACOB SHALL BE IN THE MIDST OF MANY peoples, like dew from the Lord, like showers on the grass, that tarry for no man nor wait for the sons of men.*" *Micah* 5:7

~

"WHAT DO YOU MEAN YOU CAN'T COME? WE PLANNED THIS vacation together. Now, we're in Mexico, but you brought work along? That's not fair." Lips compressing, Violet Zendel listened to her brother give what sounded like a rehearsed formal answer, quite suited to his controlled personality.

"Fine. We'll meet you back at the hotel in an hour. Meanwhile, we're stopping by this place near Highway Plaza in the old city. Tim wants to show me a nice view from there." Her voice came out tight, but she managed to contain her frustration. This was not the time to exchange words with Pete.

"See you later." She hung up, slid the phone into her back pocket, and tugged at her friend's arm. God knew she was grateful Tim Santiago came along on this vacation—their first one together in four years—or this would have turned into a work-away-from-home situation.

She lifted her gaze to his. "Pete's not coming. Let's go." With the tightness constricting her throat, even her voice couldn't hide her disappointment.

"Sorry to hear that." Tim, an eyewitness to her troubled relationship with her brother, touched her hand, lending a sense of comfort to ease the ache in her heart. Why couldn't Pete ever think of her, demonstrate, through just a little thing, like a touch of the hand, that he cared? "This way."

She followed him and lifted her chin, resolved to enjoy their last day before returning to Maryland and her college Chemistry students.

THERE WERE THREE THINGS VIOLET HATED—THE DARK, SPIDERS, and uncertainty. Yet all three were happening. Right this minute.

Crack.

She froze on the steps and spun to Tim. "Did you hear that?"

No response.

Violet gasped, then blinked against the faint lighting and inhaled the dank air in the old mansion as she lifted her leg to climb higher. She swiped at a cobweb, swiveled, but could barely make out his slim form close behind.

"Embrace your fears, Violet, and they'll turn tails and run. Don't be scared."

This was not how she heard other people's trips to ancient ruins turned out. They usually returned with memorabilia and nice photos. This didn't feel nearly relatable to those tales. Yet here she was fighting off cobwebs from her hair with almost no light to make out where next to plant her feet.

She turned to find her best friend, Tim, who now breathed close to her ear, and was standing one step below her. He smiled as she flashed her cellphone's light on him, and he blinked hard against the light. She punched his arm. "Don't laugh, Tim. It's not funny! You know I hate dark places. Why did you bring me here? And why didn't you tell me you were right behind me?"

His dark Italian curls bounced as he shook his head. "Seriously, Vi? And miss the rounded eyes that looked at me when you heard something?" Still shaking his head, he ushered her forward. "Ha. No way. Let's keep moving. We're almost there. You'll thank me for this later."

She shifted the light off his face and back on her path. "Cindy visited old Greek coliseums last year and returned with amazing photos. Now, I'll be lucky to take one picture that won't make it look like I'm lost in some underground mine and waiting to be rescued." Violet grunted but resumed climbing. As soon as she saw the top, she slowed down for Tim, who came up and stood tall next to her.

"You were excited right before we turned to climb these stairs so I'd suggest you quit complaining. Moreover," he shrugged, "maybe it was time you lost your fear of the dark."

She didn't respond, preferring to bask in the light rays and escape from the darkness. Now awash in broad daylight, she shaded her eyes from the sudden brilliance, not complaining when Tim led her toward a walkway, through which they climbed some steps to what looked like an old gallery. She dusted off cobwebs from her hair while he studied a map in his hand and switched off his cellphone's flashlight as she did hers. "You know, we could've taken the easier route the site escort offered."

"And miss out on the fun of taking the ancient way the mansion guards used in climbing up here?" Tim inched up a brow. "Nope. Not for an archeologist. We're always pursuing the secrets hidden in the dark."

"And I hate the dark." Violet sighed. "Which makes me wonder why I chose to follow an archeologist here. I could've been relaxing in the hotel with a cool drink, not crawling up holes and ruining my clothes."

Tim's laughter echoed through the old walls of the empty space as they emerged at an opening with descriptive wall plaques in the local language. "I know why you did it. Because you're my best friend. And that's what best friends do." He offered a charming smile, then dusted something off his cheek. "Come on. I'm so excited to show you a secret compartment I heard of but didn't see the first time."

"Another secret place?" She felt her eyes roll even before she spoke. "If it's dark...um...no, I don't think so."

He tugged at her arm. "Come on, Violet. There won't be dusty tunnels this time. Just stairs. Old, but well-lit stairs." He paused to allow her to choose.

She nodded. "Fine then." But she glimpsed a vivid view of the ruins of the old city walls and was drawn in by them. Crumbling bricks were hugged by beautiful green and purple-flowered shrubbery dotted with surrounding large trees. Flowers grew through the crevices of the cracked wall and lent it some strange beauty.

Violet let go of Tim's arm and approached the rectangular window. Glancing through the rough-edged window and careful not to touch it, she observed the rustic beauty. "Wow. I love this." His soft steps whispered closer on the worn carpet behind her, and for a moment, she felt a calm wave soar through her spirit. Smiling, she leaned on his shoulder and drew in a deep breath.

He curved a hand around her shoulder. "There's a reason why people leave the old to move to the new. But exploring their beginnings, and the places they abandoned, teaches me a lot about human nature. We need each other and will leave places to stay close to people we love. But you know what?"

She spun. "What?"

He let go of her shoulder. "Where a people started tells you a lot about their journey-to-become. And you can learn a lot from that."

Violet smiled. Tim had been the best thing to happen to her in recent years. He'd first asked her out, but she'd refused, knowing it wasn't God's will for them, at least, for her. She'd learned to know that every man God led into her life wasn't meant to be in a relationship with her. She asked the Lord for godly direction after meeting Tim, especially knowing she felt nothing more than friendship for him. Soon, he'd shared a choice he'd been torn about making— accepting a job offer from two different colleges across state lines.

So, they'd prayed. And after that prayer, it became clearer who God wanted Tim to be toward her—a friend and a prayer partner.

As time went by, they grew to become close friends, and then prayer partners, then travel buddies. Last year, they were both too busy to travel and had opted for Mexico this year. Violet still wasn't sure whose idea it had been to include Pete—and she'd been shocked when he'd accepted to come.

And, since Tim was soon leaving for a year as part of a South America research archeologist exchange program, she savored today's outing even more. This was the last day of their vacation, and it wasn't lost on her that, as they returned, he would begin earnest preparations for a possible return to either Mexico or South America. Truth be told, she was already missing him.

She drew in a deep breath and chose to be present in the moment. Faded paint on the old structure met with over-grown weeds and brushes to contrast beautifully with the eroded marble. She glanced up at a rusted chandelier, long past its heyday. What must have been a red-color rug beneath their feet had been worn down by time, dust, and human traffic to bare, shredded white threads at the center while spots of stubborn red color clung to the fringes.

The tall galleried room they stood in flowed into the far outside wall connected by flagstones like a well-planned palace. The owners must've been rich. Gorgeous nature wound with primitive technology provided the impetus for an appreciation of God's divine nature and how much power He gave to man on earth to build whatever he wished.

At that moment, Violet realized Tim waited for her to drink her fill of the area before leaving. So, having seen enough, she turned and followed him. He asked another person who idled by to take a photograph of them, which they graciously did before leaving the area to explore a bit more. Contrary to her expectation, with the dark stairs behind them, she was finally enjoying this. Other tourists took the longer walk from outside to come around to enter the galleria while she and Tim climbed the stairs.

At her prompt, they exited the large hall, walked down a few stone steps, and crossed a clear space toward a smaller, older ancient ruin. When they reached it, it appeared to be like a servant's quarters with narrower steps and smaller rooms than the mansion.

"It was rumored that this small place was the birthplace of the father of one of Mexico's richest families—the Nunez family—about one century ago. Although it has never been proven true."

"Interesting." She fell in step. "How old is this place then?"

He shrugged. "I'd say maybe a few hundred years old."

Luckily, some sunlight streamed in through cracks in the walls and lit up the space. The stairs, cracked in several places, seemed narrower, and the blue paint on the inner wall was faded. Holes above in the rusted zinc roofing, provided little shade from the overwhelming heat as she drank the last of her water from her bottle and tossed the container into a labeled garbage bin.

Observing the one-story structure ahead, Violet was surprised that the doors still stood and that the internal walls remained intact. It portrayed the excellence of the builders. As she approached, she noticed that the few other tourists had remained at the galleria, and some uneasiness coiled in her belly. "I don't see other tourists entering this one, Tim."

One white sign with red arrows indicated where the stairs were. He led her up the flight of steps and paused midway. "I don't see any signs saying it's out of bounds either. Come on, we won't stay here too long."

When they reached the top step, a torn, dirty curtain—the size of a sedan car window—fluttered to her left. "Tim, there's a curtain here." She stepped past him. "For such an old place, is that normal?" Surprised to see something that modern in a building so old, she approached and flipped the curtain aside with a finger.

"No, it's not normal and shouldn't be there. Any curtains should've been long gone," Tim confirmed, a worried line creasing his brow.

She peered out the window and felt her eyes widen. "What in the world...?" A dark-blue van idled afar off. Considering the crushed lawn and low wooden barricade it had crashed and driven over, it was in the wrong place.

Near it, a group of men stood in a huddle like they were trading in something secret. A heavy, black-nylon bag was exchanged for wads of cash, and just then, she saw a man standing on the other side of the window, much closer to her than the two men afar off. The curtain flapped again, his gaze met hers, and he frowned. She knew what his frown meant —she shouldn't be here.

His gray eyes bore into hers beyond the sweaty, dirt-brown scarf tied to his forehead, and something told Violet she wasn't supposed to have seen the exchange she had. A weapon clicked, and she gasped as Tim approached her and stopped. Then she felt him trailing her gaze to the weapon in the man's hands because Tim echoed her next words, "Gun!"

They ducked beneath the curtain and raced down the stairs. Being one floor up, they had an added height advantage. But bullets aiming for them bore holes into the ancient structure with thudding sounds. Either the man was using a silencer, or the walls were stronger than she thought because they weren't hit—yet. Her heart pounded in her chest, and she ran down like she was being chased by a helicopter.

"Jesus, please shield us!" Tim shouted as they exited the structure, taking the last few steps, two at a time, and landed at the outer door. Some sparsely armed security men, shouting orders to themselves, flanked the structure, and two swept past her and Tim.

She wanted to warn them that they were outgunned, but she froze when she heard a whimper. A boy, no more than six, crouched low playing with some pebbles at the edge of the structure. With his trembling lips, he seemed really scared and frozen in shock. No one else appeared to notice him.

Tim grabbed her hand to lead her out as more gunshots rang out and shouting vibrated from inside the structure, but she wouldn't leave. Her heart wrapped the boy in a hug. So, she sprinted toward the side of the structure.

"Violet!" Tim shouted behind her, but she raced forward until she reached the boy.

Panting and squatting low, she sighted the fear caught in

his big brown eyes, but she didn't let it deter her. Shoving down her own fear, she extended a hand to him. "Come. Come with me. It's okay. You'll be all right."

Once his little arms wrapped around himself, he shook like the earlier fluttered curtain.

"Violet! Come over. It's getting bad," Tim shouted again above the chaos.

But she wouldn't leave without the boy. No. She won't.

She guessed his weight with a sweeping glance. Quite slender, he didn't appear heavy. So, she offered the only thing she could—her body as a shield for him. "I'm going to carry you out of here, okay? Don't be scared." Without waiting for an answer, she slung her purse like a sling bag across her shoulder. Then she bent lower and swept her arms beneath his thighs and, with a grunt, scooped him up and hefted him onto her shoulder. Loud voices coming from inside the building warred with sporadic gunshots, but she ran as fast as she could across the distance toward safety.

Jogging under his weight, she moved quickly, praying not to get hit as she managed to reach Tim, dash behind a wall in the galleria, and set the boy on his feet before an explosion rocked the smaller structure, leading them to dive for cover.

"Violet, you could have gotten killed!" Tim barked as they ducked behind the place she had stayed to admire the view not long ago.

She covered her ears. "I wouldn't leave the kid!"

He shielded the boy, who was now hugging Tim's leg.

"Neither would I, had I seen him. But that was no excuse to put yourself in danger."

They bent over for cover as another round of explosions shook the ground. They waited for a few moments until calm settled. Then Tim carried the boy, grabbed her arm, and rushed her out of the mansion, taking the stairs two at a time again. With all the noise, surely someone must've called the authorities, but Violet wasn't waiting to double-check.

They managed to exit the space completely, tumble into the street and into normalcy before catching their breaths. Soon, the wail of a police vehicle approaching disrupted the seeming normalcy. Then another, and yet another. And not long afterward, a black truck pulled up close, and police officers rushed into the mansion.

She, Tim, and the boy stepped aside to let them through. She wasn't sure about the significance of what she'd seen, but it could have been some sort of drug deal gone bust. *Thank You, Lord Jesus, for getting us out of there safely.*

Tim's shuffle caught her attention, and she jerked her neck sideways, still fraught. Then she smiled as she saw it was him. "Violet, what you did back there was incredibly brave. You saved this boy's life." He squeezed her shoulder and his Adam's apple bobbed. "While my concern was saving yours. I feel responsible for you since I brought you here." Tim set the boy down on his feet. She dusted sand off the arm of Tim's sleeve.

"It's okay, Tim." Violet swiped sandy sweat off her brow.

"I know you were worried. Thank you for looking out for me. I appreciate it. Let's go to the hotel. For starters, I could use a cool bath in this burning heat. Moreover, this was definitely not the museum or archeological visit I envisioned. This is more Indiana Jones's style, which I can definitely do without."

His wide grin worked to bring her worry down a few notches and eased her heart rate. An average-height lady in a red dress, with spiral waves of sandy-brown hair bouncing over her shoulders, rushed to them and gushed in Spanish to Tim, who replied with acceptance of her gratitude. Tim informed her in Spanish that Violet had saved the boy's life.

Despite the lady bending and holding out both hands to the boy, Violet held on tightly to him, not wishing to hand him to a stranger until she confirmed the woman's identity. She paused until she heard the boy call her mama, reach out, and smile at her before she released him. Relief swept through her as the moment had become tense, but she wasn't regretting making sure the woman was his parent first. It would've been worse rescuing him only to hand him to a complete stranger. A police officer approached and paused, speaking to the lady first.

He must've demanded an ID because she dug one out of her purse and showed it to him, plus a photo of the boy standing with her now. While she spoke with the cop and he examined the documents as well as asked her more questions, the little boy faced Violet.

He blinked sparkling brown eyes full of innocence beneath dark lashes that melted her heart into a puddle and served as his thank you to her. She dipped into her pocket and gave him a granola bar, and he stepped closer and enclosed it with eager hands, smiling wider before turning back to his mother whom the police now cleared to leave. Reunited with her son, she scooped him up into her arms and kissed his cheeks, and Violet was sure she would scarcely put him down anytime soon as they both disappeared into the street's foot traffic.

The officer interviewed them next, and after they each gave their statements, providing their names, addresses, and contact information, they were cleared to go. Soon, the area was cordoned off with yellow Do-Not-Cross tape.

Leaving them all behind, Violet and Tim returned to where he had parked a rental car. Luckily, the garage was easily accessible and not cordoned off. They paid at the meter and climbed inside the sedan. She made a mental note to add getting shot at to her list of things she hated.

She slid her seat belt across. "Well, can you make sure next time we go to a museum of any kind, we're going to be safe before we pop into a possible drug deal?" When Tim's eyes widened, she laughed as she sat up straight. "I'm joking. Well, not about the safety. But I know there's nothing you could've done about today's occurrence."

"Thanks. You had me gaping for a second. I can't get enough of your professorial attitude ever, can I?" He grinned when she opened her mouth to reply, then realized he teased and shut it again.

"One of these days, Vi." Tim eased off the curb and entered traffic, and soon they were heading toward their hotel.

Pete would hardly believe what she had just experienced when they reached the hotel and she told him.

Relieved and sure they were safe for now, she heard her phone ringing. Still catching her breath, she dug it out of her purse, pressed Answer, and raised the phone to her ear. "Hello?"

"Violet? It's Pete."

A frown pinched a curve to her eyes. "Pete?" But he rarely called, if ever. She usually did the calling.

"Yes." Her brother came through rather coolly, a contrast to the situation she had just encountered.

"Is everything okay, Pete?" She pressed a hand to block her ear against a loudly-tooting horn from a car nearby. But the next words weren't what she expected.

"There's been an emergency. I need you to return right away." A slight pause followed, and Pete wasn't the pausing type.

That got her heart pounding again. And scared.

3

"In that day, the Lord of hosts will be for a crown of glory and a diadem of beauty to the remnant of His people." - Isaiah 28:5

~

Angel Martinez used the back of her hand to wipe condensation from her windshield as she veered off the highway exit at two in the morning. Thankful to be heading home—finally—she resisted the urge to massage the stiffness gripping her neck. Well, considering the cases she was handling, her unease was like small change. It had been enough that a local psychiatrist ended up dead in a suspicious accident on the same day her assistant narrowly survived dying in a fire. As she read the cases, hard as she tried, she couldn't fashion a reason for the arson or for the murder. The names of the possible suspects they had so far hadn't shaken anything loose, nor had the victim's birthplaces nor anything else given a clue as to the identities of the architects of these crimes. With time, something would give, but when?

She navigated past the slow car, wondering if the driver was falling asleep at the wheel considering his tires wobbled between lanes. While she passed him and flashed her police cruiser lights briefly as a warning, he straightened up in his lane and sat up, giving her a generous smile. A nod sufficed for a polite response before she returned her sight to the road. The ringing of a phone drew her attention back to her vehicle, and she pressed the hands-free Bluetooth earpiece to answer. "Hello?"

"Send backup! Shots fired...Hurry." A scramble followed in the airwaves. Then the call disconnected.

"Pierce?" Angel blinked at the phone atop her purse even though she recognized her partner's voice. He'd hitched a ride with her because his car had a flat tire. Having just dropped him off at his house, she was still close enough to return.

She grabbed her radio and alerted the SSPD, and then swerved her vehicle to the shoulder until all four tires scrunched on gravel and she was free to turn.

She flipped on her sirens to full blast as she drove against the traffic until she found a safe place to join the southbound lane. Driving fast, she was soon back to the road leading to Pierce's home. She prayed he would be safe until her arrival. Within minutes, she pulled up at his driveway as the spark of gunfire lit up the dark interior.

Angel grabbed her gun, jumped out of the cruiser, and ran, head down, toward the house. The front door was unlatched, and it hung open. She pushed it wider, entered, and groped through the hallway using her hand. No other identifiable sound reached her ears, so she had to do something.

She took out her cell phone, which she'd grabbed from the car, and flicked on the light function. Then she slid it as far as she could to the other end. As though in response to her action, gunfire exploded from both the living room and the bedroom door at the end of the hallway. Angel ducked.

"Pierce! It's me. Where are you?" She had to know so she wouldn't hit the wrong target. Once during their training years ago, she had mistakenly hit a camouflaged target and had learned her lesson then. Now was not the time to risk her partner's life.

"Over here!" echoed.

Good. He was still alive. "To the living room then," Angel muttered. She would risk getting hit by the shooter from the open bedroom doorway if she attempted to cross while standing. So, she trotted to the edge, dove across, and landed with a hard hit on the living room floor. Gunfire shot past her, but she had been quicker. Her partner's rapid breathing whizzed as police sirens whirred close by. She peered at him in the darkness, then whispered, "What happened? Are you okay?"

"I came in and saw this guy robbing my house. He was unplugging the TV about to cart it away. Clearly, I had surprised him, and he didn't know I was a cop. He panicked and shot first, and I ducked. Then I flipped the lights off from the control. But we clashed. As I turned to call you, he lunged at me, and I lost the phone. He ran to the bedroom and hid there. We've been exchanging fire since then."

"God be praised, you're still alive." Angel felt for his feet and heard him wince. "Are you injured?"

"I might have taken a hit to my leg because I'm having a hard time moving it."

"Stay here." She rose to her feet but kept her head low. "I'll try to draw him out."

"Please be careful."

"Okay." She moved one step closer to the hallway listening for any sounds. Before she could take another step, an object hit her back, and she fell.

It was the shooter now leaving the bedroom.

She lunged at him in the shadows and kicked the gun from his hands, which she could see from the reflecting light from her cellphone afar off. Then she flipped onto her back, pointed the gun, and froze. She couldn't tell why, but all of a sudden, it was her and her first foster parent again. The images flashed in her mind.

Him towering above.

Her struggling underneath.

Then the gun in her hands went off.

Angel shuddered but managed to shake the trauma from her mind long enough to see the attacker dive toward her. She swung her leg, and it made contact with his jaw. He groaned, then began struggling for her gun. The door burst open, and other police officers had arrived. Lights flashed around them, but the struggle continued.

"Police!"

"Over here!" Pierce shouted as the place flooded with lights. The officers closed in. Soon, seeing her uniform, an officer shot the attacker in the back, and he slumped on her. She pushed his weight off her and rose.

"Thanks. He entered the property and was robbing my partner."

Another officer cuffed the unconscious man, while another called for an ambulance.

"Pierce is injured so we need two ambulances."

She slid over and sat up against a window, breathing hard. "I need someone to unmask him so we'll see his face."

An officer standing close by did so. Then he flipped the man onto his back, and she took a look—short brown hair, narrow nose, and scanty brows. Satisfied, she leaned back and waited for the officers to process the scene.

It was going to be a long night.

4

"For there is nothing hidden which will not be revealed, nor has anything been kept secret but that it should come to light."
–Mark 4:22

Two days later, Angel sat in her office at the SSPD and lifted her eyes when she heard someone approaching. She blinked, sure she was seeing double. Her brother stood in the front of her office, and, a moment after her shock wore over, she beckoned with a wave for him to enter. She pushed back her chair and almost sprang to her feet, eager to go over and hug him. But considering the last time they saw each other—the day he called her a hateful, religious freak—was the same day he left town, she wasn't sure how well that hug would go over. So, she simply settled for a question. "John? What are you doing here?"

Hit by a throbbing headache, she rubbed her forehead as he took the seat opposite her desk. His rugged blue jeans were washed out, his orange T-shirt could use a round in the washing machine, and his disheveled hair needed an introduction to a comb. Was he homeless? Refusing to make assumptions, she waited for him to state his mission. She set down the file she was working on and locked her PC's screen and faced him fully.

He clasped his hands. "I hope you don't mind me coming here."

She eyed his short hair and rough beard but said nothing. It was barely three years since the last time they saw each other. Ten years her junior, John had grown so tall it was impossible to spot any age differences between them unless you were close to their family. But at only twenty-two, he had aged more than he should. "Sure."

"That's fine. How can I help you?" She wove her hands together and settled them on the desk, fighting back an exhausted yawn stemming from the attack two days ago. Going to the hospital and rotating between stopping at the floor where her partner was being treated and the floor where the attacker was in custody had worn her out.

So had giving her statement and writing up and submitting her report, which had pretty much consumed the better part of yesterday morning. She'd gone home, showered, changed her clothes, and then returned to the hospital after buying Pierce food. Since he was a widower, no one was taking any meals to him. He had appreciated it. Then she headed to the station to dig further into her current murder case.

Luckily, the girl who'd survived the fire had woken up and given her statement. Without her seeing the arsonists' faces, Angel was almost thrust back to the start.

"I'm here because I need your help." John appeared to hold his breath while waiting for her answer. Then his gaze dipped.

"John, what's the matter?"

Finally, the yawn escaped. Obviously, her last cup of coffee had washed down her belly without doing its job—working to keep her awake. Next, her eyelids would likely be drooping. But she wasn't leaving until she made some headway on this case—and heard her brother out.

"I..." He pinned his gaze to a point past her head. "I need a place to stay. For now."

She felt the frown deepen her brows. "Why?"

His Adam's apple bobbed. "I got into a situation and...I lost all my money and my house."

Angel crossed her arms. "What kind of situation?"

He studied his open palms. "Gambling. I moved to Vegas. Me and the guys were out one night, and we went to the casino. One thing led to another, and before we knew it, it became a habit." He ran a hand through his hair. "Listen, if you can't help me, that's fine. But can I crash on your couch for a few days until I figure things out?"

She stayed silent as she thought through his revelation and reeled at the level of indiscipline.

"Please?" In the past, John didn't apologize or beg. He simply took and walked away when things got tough. For him to beg her now, he had to be desperate.

"Fine. But you need to apply for and get a job soon."

His shoulders slacked and he nodded. "I will."

Based on his recent revelation, she didn't have to ask about his credit score. It might be hard for him to find a decent job. "You might want to look at construction companies that could be hiring. They could hire you more quickly."

"Okay, I will." He stood and wiped his likely sweaty palms on his jeans. "And thank you."

She reached for her purse, stood as well, and dialed her supervisor. "I need to go to my house for an hour. I have a family emergency." After giving him a brief explanation, she walked out with John in tow.

Their parents had died when they were young. Of all her siblings, John was the most troublesome. He had been hard to tame when they were younger, living with their foster parent who beat them up when he got high—until the day he'd called her names, then tried to strangle her with his belt and she shot him with his own gun. She'd been afraid to report him to authorities, fearing her siblings might get split up. That was when her life changed irreversibly. Luckily, they found someone who wanted all of them in their home. Since then, she was basically the parent to her four siblings and had managed to get them settled in various jobs. The youngest had graduated college last year and was working as a computer analyst in some tech company. One was a banker. The other, a truck driver.

By God's grace, every one of them was settled in life career-wise, except John. Did he suffer because he found her sobbing after shooting their foster father who'd tried to strangle her while high, thinking she was his ex? Angel wasn't sure. She just knew that, from that time onward, John had changed. He was more aggressive, didn't listen to instructions, joined some street gangs, and it had taken sustaining a gunshot wound to make him accept to go back and finish school. She'd thought the nightmare was over.

Yet here he was today with a new tale.

How long would she have to carry him? He was not a Christian. And praying for him and his conversion to Christ had been at the top of her agenda. But she was feeling like God wasn't ready to answer her yet, and she was tired of praying for it and seeing things get worse and not better.

Even when they were moved to a foster home with absentee parents and a middle-class paycheck, she had delayed her own dreams of going to college and worked night jobs to help her siblings out. By the time she finished supporting the last sibling to start college, she had turned thirty and had no time to pursue a relationship. But four years earlier, she'd admitted to herself that she couldn't handle the waitress jobs and the inconsistent hours any longer, so she applied to join the police force.

Surprised by her acceptance, she filled out the form and had smiled sadly as she circled Single yet again. Now, years later, many could not understand how she was single at almost thirty-one. But she couldn't explain that she had been too busy raising her siblings to think of having a relationship. Since her youngest sibling just finished school and started her own life, Angel was excitedly looking forward to settling down. But would she have to put her life on hold again to help out John?

She started her car, and as John buckled up, she turned to him. "Listen, I know you might not understand this, but each time you get into criminal behavior, you set the timer of your life backward. Aren't you tired of playing catch-up? Won't you ever change?"

She gripped the wheel with desperate hands, willing them to change someone they couldn't. "Look around you. No one is here to help you. So next time someone tempts you into doing something wrong, ask yourself whether they will stand with you when everything hits the fan? Only Jesus stands with you through thick and thin, whether you like to hear it or not."

She tapped a finger on her chest. "Do you think I'm here because I'm better than you? I've been single all these years, and I've not yet faced a problem that God allowed to overwhelm me even with my imperfections. Do you think it's by my own power that I was able to support you, Stephanie, Grace, and Hughes?" She shook her head. "Of course not. Without the grace of God, we wouldn't have made it, John. So, I'm asking you to take a minute and think about where your life goes from here. If you continue in this path and end up in jail, I can't help you."

He simply sat there and said nothing. So she started the car, revved the engine, and drove from the lot, hoping and praying she could scale this new challenge with John, without losing her patience with God.

Between the murder case, her partner's robbery, and John's fresh issues, could she handle anything else? Why did she fear things had just begun?

5

"But I would strengthen you with my mouth, and the comfort of my lips would relieve your grief." –Job 16:5

For a day of visiting an old mansion and getting shot at, Violet was sure she could handle one bad event for one day. But another? Certainly no.

She'd waited on the phone, and her brother, Pete, had stayed silent until she could take it no more. "Pete?"

Whatever he had to say wouldn't he just say it? Or better yet, did she truly have to hear it?

Silence, heavy with apprehension, hovered like a dark cloud full of ominous rain.

"What is it?" She swallowed hard and waited for what felt like another full minute, though it might've been only a couple of seconds. "Tell me. I can handle it." Maybe she could handle it, but she couldn't shake the dread filling her.

Tim nudged her arm. "Is everything okay with Pete?"

She squeezed his hand near her arm before he returned it to the steering wheel and smiled but said nothing, waiting for her brother to speak when he felt able to get his words out. This was highly unusual for him. He was pretty much a say-your-mind-and-get-it-over-with kind of guy.

"Dad is dead."

Violet blinked, her vision a blur as her world spun off its edge. "Pete?" She clasped her forehead.

Did she hear him right? "No."

"I'm sorry, Vi. He's gone." An echo of his words chilled over her sunburned skin like a block of ice.

Her dad was fine. He had to be. "He wasn't sick when we left the States, Pete."

"I know. But something happened, and they couldn't catch it in time the doctors said." The last time his voice got this grainy was when their mom had passed. He had been close to their mom, even though he would have nothing to do with her faith in Christ.

"What are you saying, Pete? What happened to Dad?" Her ears rang with the words, and she wished some horn would toot and blast the words away with them. She felt her fingers clench the dashboard as she hunched over and settled her head there. Something had to feel real here beyond the pain rising in her heart and threatening to drown her.

"It was a brain aneurysm. They said he collapsed while walking in the community garden. Someone found him and called an ambulance. They took him to the hospital and suspect no foul play, but they couldn't do anything to help him. It was...just too late. He's gone, Vi."

But she was no longer listening.

"No." She pounded her fist on the dash and wished she had gotten the call. She would've insisted they do more. "They can't say it's too late. They can try something, anything," she pleaded, weariness burying the tail of her words while pain swelled in her heart. "Dad can't be dead. I refuse to believe it."

"I'm sorry, Violet. So sorry," Tim whispered to her ear as he flicked the blinker and parked by the roadside curb beside a shoe store.

"I pushed them for more details, and they said it's been twenty-four hours already. They tried to verify his identity when he was first brought in. Then they reached out to those who'd taken him to the hospital. It took some time, hours later, before someone knew who he was, but he had been pronounced dead by then. He's been gone for twenty-four hours already."

She almost challenged Pete further, but she would be blaming the wrong person. It was indeed too late. Pete knew how much their dad meant to her, and he wouldn't have called her if it wasn't true.

"Noooo. No. No." Her voice grew weaker with realization. Her world had just shattered. The phone fell from her trembling hand, tumbled to the floorboards while sobs wracked her body. She didn't know when Tim came around the car and opened her door. She simply felt his strong arms wrapping around her shoulder and drawing her in as she wept.

Her hero was gone.

Angel stepped out of her patrol car and slammed the door. Eyeing the law offices of Sanderson and Curtman, she approached the redbrick building. With it tucked away at the other end of town, it had taken almost an hour to drive down here. But Reggie Sanderson had been the last man to see Miranda Sow alive, and Angel was going to find out why the late psychiatrist had visited him that afternoon. And if that had anything to do with her death.

She reached the doors at the second floor, pressed the bell, and waited. Soon, a receptionist with blonde hair opened the door, flashed a smile, and swung the door wider to allow her entry.

"Welcome to Sanderson and Curtman. Please have a seat, and someone will be with you shortly."

"I'm here to see Mr. Sanderson on an official police matter." Angel took a seat between two offices facing each other with one receptionist desk at the center. Soon, someone emerged, and based on the DMV records she'd checked, it had to be Mr. Sanderson. But she waited until he drew close and identified himself.

The short man with double-rimmed glasses and a bald center on his head extended her a hand. After introducing himself, he led her into a spacious office where bookcases full of tomes lined both sides of the wall. Long bookcases covered all areas of the office, scarcely leaving space for a walkway or desk or chair. "Please, have a seat."

Angel sat down, focusing on the framed photo on his desk of him and a young boy playing soccer. He didn't appear to be much older than she was. And suddenly, she yearned for a husband and child of her own. Seeing her peers married and living with their own spouses and kids raised a desire in her. But she was also aware of the uniqueness of her situation. She knew God was in control and would sort her out at His time.

She tore her eyes away from the image to the man himself. "Yes, I'm Officer Martinez. And I'm here about Miranda Sow. My understanding is that she came to see you a couple of days ago. Can you tell me what that visit was about?"

He clenched his mouse and stopped moving it. Then his gaze darted toward the door, and his Adam's apple bobbed.

"I'm sorry, but is Miranda in any trouble? Does she require legal representation?"

"Miranda is dead. She was killed in a hit and run—run off the road in what appears to be a deliberate attack. We're trying to determine why she was killed and by whom."

Color drained from his face, and she edged forward in her leather chair. "You can help us by telling me why she came to see you."

"Dead? Truly? She was just here... hale and hearty." He shook his head, scratched a short beard, and then met her gaze with resolve. "Miranda came to me and asked if she would be able to retain my services in case someone was targeting her."

"Did she say who?"

He nodded. "She said she thought she might be in danger. At first, she wouldn't say who she suspected. But I convinced her our conversation was confidential."

Angel cleared her throat, wanting him to conclude faster. "Interesting story. Do you have the name of the individual in question?"

He hesitated. "You did not hear this from me."

A frown twisted her face. "Why? Who is he?"

"Richard Danielson III. She said he might be the one, though I doubt it."

Angel blinked. Then her eyeballs rounded. "The congressional candidate? Son of Congressman Danielson II?"

He nodded. "One and the same."

"Wow. What was Miranda's connection to him?"

He stared at her. "I was too shocked to ask. I just told her to come back when she had more evidence."

"What evidence did she share, if any?"

"A postcard. Mailed from a high school up north. Very tidy lettering said, 'Remember us?' She shoved it back into her purse and didn't share anything more. Frankly, I figured she was just too scared. I could see it in her eyes, like she was reliving a nightmare. I thought a few days away from her job would do her good. But I told her to go to the cops if she felt unsafe or took the threat seriously."

"Unfortunately, she ran out of time." Angel equally nodded and rose. "Thank you very much for your assistance." She settled a card on his desk but doubted he would use it. Lawyers rarely called back, in her experience. "If you remember anything else, give me a call."

He stood and shook her hand. "Of course."

With those words, she left Sanderson, sure that she now had some direction for her investigation. But once she drove off the lot, she knew. If she was going to get the criminals involved in Miranda's murder and the arsonists behind bars, she had to hurry. Or she might run out of time—especially if they were powerful politicians with things they'd rather keep hidden.

If they had killed Miranda to hide evidence, they'd be willing to do it again, and she'd likely be their next target if she got too close to the right answers.

AFTER WORKING HARD ON HER CASES THAT AFTERNOON, ANGEL pushed back her chair and drew in a deep breath, breathing in the scents of stale coffee and paper—the banana peel from her makeshift lunch rotting in the trash can definitely didn't help settle the frustration swirling her stomach. Nothing had given way to corroborate the lawyer's story. She couldn't go to a congressional candidate's office with an accusation or suspicion of murder—or anything else—without facts and corroboration. She had to find a connection between Miranda and the congressman, who was several years her junior.

Was there something she overlooked? She scooted closer to the desk and studied the files before her again, determined to figure things out, even if it was a loose thread.

An hour later, she paused everything and made herself a cup of coffee to keep her awake after another long night the previous day. She soon needed another and allowed the next cup of coffee to sluice down her throat before attempting to read anything else.

She settled back in her chair, both hands wrapped around the mug. She could use some reorganization. Files were growing at a fast pace, now stacked one atop the other on the right side of her desk. Matter of fact, she smirked, the seats were the only empty spaces.

With her partner out of commission, her work had

doubled. A reminder popped up on her screen, alerting her to proceed to interview the building manager of the burned building tomorrow. Her partner's notes mentioned the manager had been away both times Pierce had checked on the man. Luckily, the scribbled address on the notepad showed a place not too far from the station.

Angel headed to the office fridge for the sandwich she'd brought for lunch, then called her brother to see how his job applications were coming.

"I applied to ten places today," John said, some lightness lacing his voice. "I already got a call from one asking about references. May I use you as my reference?"

She returned to her office, sat down with her meal, and thought about it. "No, I don't think family members can refer you, or at least, I doubt personal references are taken very seriously. I can, however, call the supervisor of the burger place you'd worked at over the summer a few years ago. He lives in the area, and we attend the same church. I'll explain your situation, and we'll go from there."

"Okay. I'll wait to hear from you before calling them back. Thanks."

"You're welcome. See you later." Angel hung up and hoped her friend, Tim, would be willing to help. Granted, John hadn't been the model employee, but Tim was the only option he had now. For her sake, he'd probably help John. Maybe, after this, John would make empowering choices and stay out of trouble. Her ability to support him in these situations was wearing thin. She could only do so much before her hands failed her.

Angel hadn't spoken to Tim for a couple of weeks. She finished eating her lunch and dialed.

"Hello?" his familiar voice answered.

"Tim, it's Angel Martinez. Do you have a minute to talk?"

Rustling sounded over the speaker. "Please hold for one moment."

She waited until he returned to the call. "Sorry if I'm interrupting something. I can call back."

"No, that won't be necessary. It's good to hear from you. I'm in church, attending a funeral, so I had to step outside. Please continue."

"You remember my brother, John? He left town about two years ago but had worked with you."

A chuckle sailed through, slightly easing Angel's tense heart. "Of course, how could I forget him? Is he okay?"

Hmmm... How should she frame things, without lying and without disclosing the whole story? "Physically, he's fine. But otherwise, not really."

"How so?"

"John showed up at the station yesterday, having lost all his money due to some gambling. I'm housing him temporarily, but he needs a job. And he's applied to a couple of places, but now, they need a recommendation. Usually, they ask for two, but it seems they would like him to start soon so they can accept one referral. Would you be willing to provide it? He'd be grateful." She paused then, as she unwrapped her sandwich and eyed wilted lettuce, added, "I know he wasn't a model employee. But right now, he's flat on his back and could use a good word in his favor."

"You don't need to worry, Angel. I will provide him with a recommendation. It won't be glowing, but he will have a good enough chance to get the job. Tell him I'm inviting him to fellowship, and maybe, he might pick up a few things to help him reshape his choices. I should clarify that this isn't a condition for helping him, more like an addition so he can get his life permanently on the right path."

A thrill shot through Angel's tired mind and chased away her exhaustion. She gripped the phone tighter and wished she could hug Tim. "Thank you so much. Tim, you're a great friend."

"And you're an awesome sister. Everyone here knows you literally raised those kids like they were your own."

"I appreciate your kind words." She flicked a dollop of mustard from the edge of the bread and reached for a napkin. "Thanks a lot."

"You're welcome. Please pass along my contact information to John for requesting the recommendation, and I'll talk to you later."

"Sure, I'll do that. And sorry for interrupting the funeral."

"No problem. A close friend's father passed away unexpectedly, though he was an old man."

"I'm sorry for your loss. Goodbye, Tim."

"Thank you. Bye, Angel."

As soon as she hung up, Angel lifted her eyes upward. *Thank You, Jesus.*

She dialed John next and gave him the update. She could hear the excitement in his voice.

"Oh, man. Thank you. I will call him and email him the recommendation request form. Thanks, sis."

"You're welcome. Don't mess this up. I have no one else to call on your behalf," she warned, sandwich still in hand, but not a bite in her stomach.

"I won't. Thank you."

"He also said to invite you for fellowship. An invitation you might want to respond to when you speak with him. I'll leave that choice between you two."

Silence followed. "I will go. I will accept his invitation to attend the fellowship."

"Oh, okay." Wow, had he really accepted to go for the fellowship? What a pleasant surprise. She wasn't even sure which fellowship it was for—men's fellowship, weekly Bible study, or another—but that didn't dampen her joy. Considering she'd invited John several times and he'd turned her down, this was one serious miracle. "I'll see you later."

"Okay, thanks again."

She wrapped up the call, checked the time, and exhaled, pushing back her chair—her small break was over. So, leaving the sandwich uneaten, she pulled her purse and her coat off the wooden coat rack then headed out to interview the girl who'd survived the fire. Maybe, with a chat, she could jog her memory a bit and unveil some new information, which might give her a sense of who Miranda had been afraid of the day she died.

6

~

ONE WEEK AFTER HER DAD HAD PASSED ON, VIOLET REMAINED in shock. In her heart, she could still hear her dad's authoritative but trusting voice echo through the waves that splashed from the river and ended where her feet wiggled into the sandy bank. *What I love about Jesus is that His death is as powerful as His words. His resurrection as renewing as His creation of the world. His power is loving and gentle, but also fierce.*

Coolness, as determined as the memory weaving through her, covered her toes. *You can trust Him, especially in those times when you're in pain or hurting. Always lean on Jesus, my daughter. He's big enough to carry you, dear. His arms are sure larger than mine.* Her dad's words filtered through the waves of memory into her hurting soul as she stood on the same shores where they had spent so many sweet family moments.

"Lord Jesus, I miss Dad and Mom, even though she's been gone for a while. I love them so so much," she swallowed past a choked throat, "and this hurts badly. I feel totally...alone without them here. I know they're with You, but is it selfish that I want them here with me?"

Violet shivered against a cool breeze wafting over her skin. Then she stared beyond the shimmer of the rising sun cast over the face of the calming water. Overcome, she sighed, wishing away what had to be done—what had to happen today.

She wove her hands together. "I'm crawling through pain, Lord, and I'm just breathing in and out and hoping this numbing pain would go away." She bowed her head as another bond of sorrow roped around her heart and she pressed a hand there to ease the knot. "I came here to draw strength to get through this event. Please help me, Lord, because I can barely stand, let alone speak a word without choking up. Grace me. Please." She drew in a long breath, then exhaled.

Moments later, and feeling slightly less burdened, she bowed her head and prayed again. "Dear Lord Jesus, every fiber of feeling, every thread of thought, and every challenge that today represents, I surrender fully to You." She raised her hands above her head. "Like Dad said to do, I give it all. Even though I don't understand why he had to go, I choose to trust You."

Her father—Paul Zendel—the now-late CEO of the Cortexe Corp., was a Christian, saved and baptized with the Holy Spirit, a God-fearing man. At this time, nothing else mattered. Knowing he was now at rest at the bosom of the Father lent her peace of mind. And she knew it with certainty.

It is well with my soul. She drew in a deep breath again and felt the burden of sorrow ease a little more. She picked up a white rock washed by the waters lapping against it near her feet. She ran a thumb over its smooth edges and managed a small smile. Her dad used to pay her in quarters with each smooth stone she picked when she was little, stones like David had in Scripture. He said it was good that she worked for her money, and that had ingrained good values into her at an early age. She learned not to take anything for granted. Holding the stone now tightly in her palm, balled into a fist, soothed her heart—which felt heavier than the object.

Catching some movement from the left, she spun toward the brushes leading back to the family cottage. Footsteps followed behind the trees, and soon, her driver emerged on the footpath, approaching her. She shifted away from him, not yet ready to go. He seemed to get the message and stopped a few yards away.

She still had one memorabilia in her pocket to digest before she faced today. She reached into her pocket and brought it out. Violet cradled the fifteen-year-old picture in her hand and swallowed hard at the faces staring back at her.

All so happy and so united. All she had left of the four persons in that picture—Dad, Mom, Pete, and herself—was Pete, and he was far from being counted as her person right now. He'd grown even more distant in the past week, even though she needed him more now.

He was her twin.

We were supposed to be best friends forever. But that was now in the past too.

A drop of rain splashed on her hand and drew her attention back to the picture. She studied the joy on her parents' faces. Her mom's long, dark hair had swept over part of her own face but nothing could hide the joy in Violet's lively eyes. It was the best family vacation she could remember. This was their family's trip to see the Northern Lights in Alaska. She had been so enraptured by such display from nature that a love for science was born in her. There she decided to study science, to seek to understand the beauty of God's universe. And Pete had enjoyed it too. He was truly her brother then, ever so protective. She had treasured this photo so much that it stayed by her bedside even now.

Violet circled a finger around her dad's smiling face near

her mom's. She sniffed back a tear and lowered her hands. "Dad, I'm going to miss you." Her heart felt heavier with each word she uttered. "I look forward to seeing you again in heaven. Adieu, Papa." With those words streaming through trembling lips, she tucked the photo into her pocket, then glanced at the smooth stone she still held.

Well, learning from her Bible, she knew something could still be done with a smooth stone. She walked over to the old tree that stood weathered against time by the riverbank and found what she'd hoped was still in a Ziploc bag nailed to a meet of two large branches. She tugged at the head of the nail, and soon, it eased loose, rusted but strong.

She opened the package, pulled out the old wooden slingshot, and smiled. Testing the rubber tied to both ends, she knew it would still work. So, she pinned the bag to the tree with the nail, and walked back to the beach, watching the current.

She tucked the smooth rock in her hand into the ten-year-old slingshot she and Pete had made and left on a tree hump many years ago and shot it over the crystal-blue waters. It landed with a thudding splash and sounded as decisive as the choice she was faced with. Today was the day she dreaded. And she would face it with faith and courage, not fear or dread.

A familiar voice broke through her thoughts. "Ma'am, we have to leave for the funeral. We're cutting it close with the time." Her driver drew closer. Usually, he stayed in the car.

But not today. Everything and everyone was out of sync. She could hardly think through the coming event without tears clouding her eyes. How was she supposed to know that the last time she saw Dad would be the last time, *ever*, on this side of eternity?

Violet swiped a stray tear and nodded even as she felt a hand on her back. She spun and, through a misty gaze, saw her driver had drawn even closer.

The gray-haired man's face crinkled with a warm smile, and understanding shone in his eyes. With one hand gently on her back, he nodded. "I'm so sorry for your loss, ma'am. Your father was a good man. I'll miss him, and so will everyone at the company. But, so we don't get people worried...we really have to go now." Always a kind man, he had picked her up from school a couple of times when she was younger, so he was no stranger to her.

Appreciating his caring attitude, she swallowed hard, shoved aside the memories of the sweet times her family had enjoyed, including the ones on this private beach, choosing to treasure it in her soul, and turned fully. "Thank you, Mr. Raison."

He lifted her purse off the ground where she had set it on the stone walkway a couple of steps away while she slid her toes into her shoe, and shoehorned the back with a finger. The stone cottage hugged the grassy plain surrounding it, well maintained year-round by the groundskeeper. A tip of its brown curved roof peeked in the distance, and the warmth inside beckoned to her.

Clutching her sweater to ward off a slight chill, she strode with equally heavy steps back to the cottage, to get ready for her ride to the church, while hoping she could still wake up and find out she had been dreaming.

Ready or not, it was time to bury her dad.

7

"...But with the temptation, [God] will also make a way of escape...." -1 Corinthians 10:13

Her visit the previous day to see Miranda's office assistant who'd survived the fire had yielded no new leads, so Angel hoped this trip across town to the building manager would lessen her frustration. She wasn't ready yet to actively pursue the angle of the congressman. Especially without any proof.

She had to find a connection, but despite searching through DMV records all day yesterday, phone numbers, and addresses listed, she could find no connection between both individuals. But if there was a possible link, then someone knew something, and she wasn't going to rest until she found out who and what.

When Angel arrived, a lady stood locking the lone office door.

"Excuse me." Angel hustled forward. "Is this the office for Spencer Leasing?" And why was she locking the door? Angel checked her watch. It was barely two p.m.

The brown-skinned lady jerked at her words, and the keys fell from her hand. Angel waited for her to pick them up and straighten before she asked again. "Can I see Mr. Spencer?"

"He...we're closed," she stuttered and swallowed.

"Closed? Are these your normal hours of operation? You always close at two every day of the week? Or did something happen?" Angel pressed a hand on her hip.

The lady darted her gaze. "No. I mean, it's complicated."

Angel staggered her stance to show she wasn't leaving. "I'm listening."

The lady swallowed again. "Officer, I promise I don't know anything. I only do what my boss tells me. I think it's better you speak to Mr. Spencer himself. He should be at his house."

Angel observed her narrowly. "His address?"

"Homestead Court—3210 Homestead Court."

Angel walked back to her cruiser and set the address into the GPS. She arrived there within twenty minutes and parked some distance away then sat there, cautious as she observed the home for movement. Seeing none, she drew closer on foot. When she reached the front door, she radioed her location and status to the station before knocking. Soon, someone shuffled to the door and peeped through the peephole. With the pause that followed, she was sure the only reason he cracked the door open was due to her uniform.

"Yes?" A short man with razor-fine hair darted his gaze to the street beyond her.

"Mr. Spencer?" she prompted.

"Yes. How may I help you?"

"I'm Officer Angel Martinez. I have a few questions about the fire on 210 West Forest Valley Road and the accident that occurred not far from it."

His Adam's apple bobbed before he opened the door wider.

She stepped into an affluent home, and her boots clicked on the hardwood. Pieces of original vintage art decorated the dining room wall while white leather chairs and a cozy-looking gray leather couch occupied the living room.

He strode toward the center of the living room and curled his arms. "You shouldn't have come. Now, they will come after you too."

She walked toward where he stood, then paused as he drew to a stop. "Who are *they*?"

His lips curved upward. "It's complicated."

"Same thing your secretary said." Angel tipped her chin.

"How so?"

"I was warned not to leave my house and to tell no one about it." He beckoned her to follow. "I don't know about the accident or the fire, what caused it." He led her to a home office near the living room, the plush white carpet softening his steps. "But..." He pulled out a file and handed it to her. "Not long ago, we were notified about pests and mold being present in that building, and we scheduled a visit with State authorities. At the time, the correspondences for this request all looked legitimate."

He sank into a black swivel chair, and judging from the circles around his eyes, he had clearly not been sleeping well.

"So, what happened?" Angel pressed a hand to the glistening desk.

He sighed and moved his mouse. "I grew suspicious when they asked for keys to the building and for unescorted inspections. But afraid to lose my business, I gave in."

"That isn't standard protocol, I assume?"

"No, far from it." He shook his head. "We usually send a staff member or two to follow them and monitor the process and record any findings so we can fix anything they uncover."

He shook his head, and a frown dented the side of his mouth. "Little did I know, they weren't from the State, that instead they had duplicated the keys and returned to the building the next day."

"The day of the fire."

"Yes." He wiped a hand over his face, the rasping sound of his stubbled jaw grating her nerves. "Then I was warned to make sure I told no one about it, which I didn't because they said they will burn down my house too. And not to leave my house, which I haven't. But I had my secretary call the State to verify, and they said there was no scheduled inspection according to their records. It was all fake, even though the notification letter arrived with original stamping. I have no idea how they got it. I almost called the cops, but..." He shrugged. "I love my family. They warned me the next day not to contact the State office again, so someone in there could be collaborating."

He closed his eyes, puffing a slow breath across thick lips. "I'm so confused. But one thing I'm sure of—the people behind this are powerful and seem well-connected. A vehicle makes rounds of my house a couple of times a day... perhaps just so I know they're watching me closely. What I don't know is how or who."

Well, she was starting to have a good idea. She pushed away from the desk and paced a few steps before facing him again. Yep, she had a lot of random info being thrown at her from more sources, and yet she just had no proof. How was she to figure all this out? She started with the question uppermost in her mind. "Do you know why the psychiatrist was targeted? Did anything stand out about her? Was there anything saved from the fire that we can take a look at?"

Angel didn't wish to scare him with her rapid-fire questions, but she also needed as much information as possible.

Spencer powered down his PC. "No, I'm not sure what ax they had to grind with her. She seemed like a really nice lady. Been in that building for more than seven years." He rounded the desk and paused. "The fire department saved a major portion of the last room in her office, the one housing client files. I guess you can look at the file cabinet with the list of her clients. They were in the back and untouched by the fire, save some smoke damage."

"Yes, please, I'd like that."

Stunned at the unraveling events, Angel began to wonder whether the answer to the woman's murder lay somewhere within those files. Her client list would be a great place to start. Thoughtfully, she straightened and approached the window.

Just before she reached it, a boom ruptured the quiet outside, and she peered through a crack between the curtains. Her cruiser was on fire. A second explosion rocked her cruiser—the only vehicle left in the front street-level curbside parking—and then the lights inside the house went out. She dove beneath Mr. Spencer's desk, pulling him down with her. His phone rang, and he picked up the call, then hung up.

"They said I shouldn't have called the cops." His voice shook. "They know you're here. They said they will..."

She pressed a hand to her lips. "Shhh. I never swallow an

enemy's threats. Come with me. What's the farthest room from the entrance?"

"The kitchen. It leads out to the backyard."

Angel dialed the station as he led her, guided by natural lighting. Thankfully, they reached there safely, and she got her captain on the line. "Please send for backup. Someone blew up my cruiser and threatened to burn the property manager's house down. Also, send a team to retrieve the file cabinet with the deceased victim's files. Our answers could be in there." She dictated her current address again, just to be sure they had it, and was told to sit tight until help arrived.

But she wouldn't stay idle.

She led the man to duck near the edge, away from the kitchen door, then realized she'd forgotten to tell the captain where in the house she and the man were hiding. On second thought, she figured they might leave their current location if forced to, and so she didn't bother.

"Were you close to her? I mean, Miranda? What kind of person was she?"

"We weren't personally close, no. We maintained professional contact." He managed to say, though still wide-eyed. "But she was nice. She invited me and some of our staff to a Christmas party years ago, and we met some of her clients. Some were college students. One was the owner of a hospital, and there were also some professors. It was many years ago, so the details are sketchy. Sorry, I can't recall more."

"That's okay. You're doing great. Could any of them have targeted her?"

"Honestly, I don't know. At the time, they all had high praises for her, so I hope not. I guess people can change."

She dialed the captain to update him on their location as soon as the wail of sirens echoed down the street. Then the front door burst open with a loud gunshot, and she pulled the man away to hide behind the kitchen table.

She cut the call, silenced her radio, and they both went silent. Clicking sounds trailed the shot as footsteps moved around the house. She raised her hand and grabbed a plastic bowl from the counter. Then she laid low and slid the bowl across to the kitchen door. It rested against the border between the kitchen and dining area, just where she wanted.

She hid again as voices called out threats.

Another voice took over, a female voice. "We promise to make your end quick and painless." Harsh laughter vibrated through the hall.

The crash of glassware, likely the ones on the dining table across from them, resounded nearby, and Angel squinted but didn't move. Another set of glassware crashed to the ground.

"The tougher you make this, the rougher it will be for you," the male intruder warned.

But the sirens were upon them now.

It was only a matter of seconds before the other police officers arrived to help. *Sixty seconds to go....*

Until then, they just had to stay alive. *Lord, please shield us.* Her host gripped her arm, causing her to turn her head. She pressed a finger on her lips, and he nodded. Then she waved for him to keep his head down, which he did, although she doubted he was planning to get up unless forced to. She pulled out her gun, disabled the safety, clutched it with both hands, and waited.

Angel crept around the left side of the table as the click of a boot approaching from the right reached her ears. She clamped the sturdy leg of a chair close to her with one hand and peered, weapon pointed first. Someone kicked the bowl she'd tossed forward—so they'd entered the kitchen. Gunfire being exchanged outside ratcheted things up, but she stayed focused.

Less than ten seconds to wait for police....

Any moment now, she would face the intruders.

The eyes of the Lord are upon the righteous and His ears are open to their cry, the Scripture worked into her conscious mind, leading her to utter another prayer in her heart. *Lord, please guide me with Your eye.* She flattened on the ground to gain an angular advantage. As she crawled on her belly to the end, all sounds ceased. Had the intruders spotted them?

She flipped on her back, and her gaze collided with that of a masked man in black-and-black towering above her, his drawn brows indicating he was still unsure if he was seeing correctly. But that bought her enough time. She shot first, then scrambled to her feet. The bullet hit his mid-thigh, and he grunted and planted a hand there.

"Run!" She pushed Mr. Spencer out the kitchen door as she spotted an officer racing toward them from behind the shooter. But the lady accomplice had the police officer within her sights.

Angel pointed ahead to warn him. "Shooter!"

The officer flipped around and shot before making a full turn, and that move saved his life and took down the female intruder. Her attacker, the man, had reversed and was reaching for his fallen gun.

She spun and raced out the door, following Mr. Spencer. Then the man must've reclaimed his gun since he returned fire, and she ducked behind the door, on the other side. *Bam! Bam. Bam.* Rapid fire echoed as the officers fired at him inside.

So, defying all odds at the risk of getting hit, she jumped up to her feet, ran across the backyard, and fled with spraying fire behind her, just as his shots grew closer like he was chasing her.

But she kept running, determined. She would escape terror or die trying.

8

"...Weeping may endure for a night, but joy comes in the morning." –Psalm 30:5

By the time Violet was dressed up and had reached the church, a limousine bearing Pete drew up and parked next to hers. They had planned to meet up this morning, if necessary, at the cottage where she'd been staying should last-minute changes or anything else crop up.

With them living on opposite sides of town and across state lines, this arrangement eased the logistics for the past week since the cottage was closest to Pete's house, only minutes away, across the river, by road. It had also given her the opportunity to relive treasured memories of their family there.

To her surprise, well-wishers had gathered in the parking lot close to the church entrance. They drew closer to offer support. Soon, she smiled at the first person, Shelby, her dad's former secretary who'd retired last year and moved out of state to live with her kids.

The silver-haired woman with a frail frame wrapped her in a hug. "Vi, dear, I'm so sorry for your loss!" Violet returned her hug and accepted the flowers as Shelby wiped tears from her cheeks with a trembling hand. Osteoporosis had turned Shelby into an indoor person, but her agility remained visible in her clear gaze.

"Thank you, Ms. Shelby. And thank you for coming." Grateful to have her driver standing close by, Violet passed him the flowers. Soon, someone else came close and hugged her, gifted her a bouquet, and then shook hands with Pete, who was idling quite some distance away. They were offered more condolences. Violet gave the flowers to her driver one more time.

Most of the small crowd were her dad's friends, former and current employees of Cortexe Corp., plus some older gentlemen who'd been among the first to join the company but no longer worked with them. She greeted everyone warmly and accepted the flowers and food they gave. The aroma of casserole sailed into her nostrils but couldn't stir hunger in her grieving belly.

More people handed her warmhearted gifts like packaged food, drinks, and so many flowers that her driver and Pete's took turns getting them all into both cars.

Her driver drew close and whispered into her ear. "We have to join the service now."

She acknowledged him with a nod, then waved to those remaining around them. "Thank you so much. We are touched by your sympathy. May God bless you. We have to go now." The crowd dispersed, and almost everyone filed ahead of her into the church.

But she couldn't get her feet to move. She stood in place, overwhelmed by the love of her community, feeling like they'd collectively hugged her. The past several days, her church family had surrounded them with their prayers and sent heartfelt emails and text messages and phone calls. That alone gave her strength to face the task ahead. Of course, she alone responded to their messages, since Pete considered those ones to be strangers. But Violet didn't mind. She worked to remain the link between her family and the church.

She made her way to Pete as her driver parallel-parked, and both siblings managed a brief nod. He squeezed her hand and swallowed hard before letting go, but his face was wound as tight as twined ropes, lines etching deeply into both sides with heavy eyelids sitting over them. The hour they had both dreaded had arrived—and if not for God's grace, she didn't feel even a tiny bit ready for it—and matter of fact, at this point, Violet figured she never would.

No one was ever ready to say goodbye to their parent, no matter how bad or good those parents were in their lifetime. Thankfully, she had only great memories of the man whom they had called Dad and of their mom. Pete waved her toward the church doors, and when she didn't move, he walked ahead of her up the steps. The sharp sound of a red-breasted sapsucker pecking at a maple tree near the church doors helped unglue her feet.

Violet held her breath and strode with heavy steps into the Christ Believers' Church. She brushed off dry fall leaves from the left shoulder of Pete's black pantsuit, which might have fallen from the maple tree. Knotting her lime-green scarf—her mom's favorite color—over her black dress more tightly, again, she wished she was dreaming. But she wasn't. Her heart ached with the loss of a man who was more than dad to her—he was her hero.

Pete's dark hair, much like their dad's, reminded her of him afresh and blurred in her vision as tears threatened to overtake her will not to cry. Though his face had seemed calm earlier, his shoulders hunched over with his obvious fresh realization of their loss. At least, his head had blocked her view from the faces watching their entrance or she would lose it completely. Today, no matter who she saw, a smile was out of the question. Sliding past the full church in attendance, she caught a few surprised brethren and friends staring at Pete. Of course, they would stare.

He hadn't entered this church in a long time, much too

long. And only their dad's funeral could've squeezed him through those oak doors. She caught his side-glance as he turned to check on whether she followed. Then satisfied, he advanced. The hardness of his countenance was only surpassed by the rugged quarter-sawn oak pew on the left aisle, which they were moving toward at the front row.

Violet managed to swallow past a tight throat, wishing for a private moment to gather her emotions but knowing that was not an option now. Having spent the better part of the night in tears, and the morning getting emotionally and physically ready, she already felt spent. And the service had barely begun.

Her voice was likely gone too, but she couldn't be sure as she had barely spoken to anyone but God since she woke. Putting her clothes on and thinking of going to bury her dad had been a struggle. But she'd forced herself up and out the door. Even the cottage had felt empty without their parents. Before leaving today, she'd glanced at a framed image inscribed with choice words from her dad's favorite poem. The art decorated the space between the entrance to the cottage and the fireplace.

She'd smiled sadly as she walked past and made a note to move it to her apartment instead of donating it like they'd decided they would do with the other items in the cottage that weren't personal effects or company property.

They'd also decided not to sell the cottage. Too many sweet memories remained there, and a stranger wouldn't appreciate its worth. What a relief to agree on that with Pete since they hardly agreed on anything the past several years, leading to the distance yawning between them—distance she alone made concerted efforts to bridge.

She also saw no need to sell furniture since she had more than enough and so did Pete, and thanks to the great foundation laid for them by their parents, they had a good life and lacked nothing. However, some of the non-furniture items in the house had sentimental value, and those they would definitely not give away. This morning she just wasn't in the right frame of mind to start putting things away, even though the moving boxes she'd ordered had arrived.

She would need some weeks off to go through everything since they'd accumulated a lot of stuff over the years. And, even without asking, she knew Pete would leave all those choices to her.

Now guided by the ushers toward their seats, Violet stopped where her name was taped to the back of a pew, entered the aisle, and sat beside Pete. She set her purse down and glanced at him. His stoic face—and square jaw still hard as granite, as it has been the past decade and a half since he came home from school a very different person—was unreadable.

Yes, biologically Pete was her twin brother. However, since he changed from being the warm, protective brother she knew, denied his faith in Christ, and grew this hardened shell, the difference was as night and day. She could easily confront Pete each time he behaved badly, but that would've put even more distance between her and her only sibling— distance she hadn't wanted.

Torn between getting him to the good side, and loving him, she'd cut him a lot of slack, which probably didn't help. Right now, she'd wished for a glimpse into what had changed her brother. But each time she dared to ask, he shut her down, *fast*.

As she faced forward and listened to the Word while tension reverberated from Pete, she shoved the rising pain downward. His stiff frame and clenched fists did more to increase her nervousness than to quell it.

In her heart, Violet was tired of being the one who worked to hide that their resemblance was simply facial. Her heart hurt each time he huffed when the Word of God was being shared, like now as his grip fastened with whitened knuckles on the ring of car keys looped on his middle finger. Or like the way he'd shifted away from her whenever they ate together, as soon as she blessed her meal before eating.

Nevertheless, she held on to hope for him, even though the more she hoped, the more it appeared like he was getting farther away from God. But no matter what, she'd keep loving him. He was her brother, and she hoped to glimpse the kind of brother he once was—a Christian, loving and caring. She hoped that day wouldn't be too much longer.

9

"Nevertheless, God who comforts the downcast, comforted us...." -2 Corinthians 7:6

～

"Amazing Grace" filtered into Violet's ears. The age-old music playing from the organ soothed her grief. Thinking about her dad, she scarcely managed to keep the tears at bay. Knowing their mom had passed some years ago made this even harder.

At the time, Pete, who was on a flight returning to the US from Spain, spoke to their mom by phone about an hour before she passed away at the nursing home where she was being cared for, due to Alzheimer's. That experience and her sudden loss were in no way comforting. They had hoped that their dad would live longer—much longer than four years afterward.

Tears disobeyed her instruction not to flow and dropped down her left cheek. Another followed as she recalled the shadow of their mom praying for Pete every night on her knees, with her head bent, after tucking Violet into bed, and often sharing a Bible story with her. Violet would pretend to be asleep.

But her mom's audible groans toward heaven remained indelible in her memory—and had seared the commission to continue praying for Pete's conversion into Violet's heart. Little did she know that until today, now with both their parents gone, Pete would still be the way he was—locked behind a glass seal where nothing spilled through—nothing.

Violet dipped her lashes and used the tip of her finger to swipe the tear dangling along the edge. At a tap on her shoulder, she lifted her gaze and met Pete's.

Her eyes dropped to his hand where he held out a fresh set of tissues. But she had spotted some softening in his glance. His brown eyes still appeared swollen, and the edges were wrinkled more than before. He was in pain too. She could see it. He just fought hard not to show it. But why? She sighed inwardly.

"You can have mine, Vi." His first words today. He swallowed hard, and his Adam's apple bobbed as she accepted them. "We'll be fine, *mi querida hermana*."

His Spanish endearment, meaning my dear sister, was his

first attempt at softness in a long time. Like an answer to prayer, it sluiced through her heart and soul, bringing a drenching of hope to the parched places within her. She replied with a nod as her long black hair tumbled over her shoulder. "Gracias."

Since she was born, Violet learned Spanish from her dad, even though the Spanish language was rarely, if ever, spoken in their house despite their Hispanic family origin.

Simply because they usually had non-Spanish speaking friends and church family members around, English became their primary language of communication. Spanish was also like their little-known secret that allowed her to hear what people said when they thought she or Pete didn't understand. On rare occasions, or during hard times like now, when communication was tough, they switched from English to Spanish.

Pete faced the altar again as the funeral service continued with songs and hymns she'd chosen from her parents' favorites, played by the choir. She managed to follow the service as eulogies of her dad were given by family friends and colleagues and an elderly aunt. As she listened, her nerves calmed until her eyes met an object placed by a minister gingerly at the center of the altar, and her gaze froze on it as he walked back to his seat.

Their dad's cremated remains in an urn stared back at her in an unreal manner. She darted her gaze away and noticed she and Pete both avoided looking in that direction as their gazes shifted rightward. She would burst out in tears if she chanced more than a glance at it. No. This wasn't how she wished to remember him. Her dad was more than what was in that container.

Violet instead allowed herself to flourish with memories of the sweet man—lively, vibrant, and jovial. Always had a smile for everyone, and never intentionally hurt anyone. Gregarious and fun to be around.

It warmed her heart how he would play soap bubbles with her as a little girl in between phone meetings with his staff whenever he worked from home. During the winter, on snow days, Dad would pull her around in a sled on snow and glue on a white beard like Santa riding on a sleigh.

Then the day after Christmas, he'd drive the entire family, in their real car, to a Christmas dinner in the city from the cottage, their Christmas home away from home. Maybe that was why the cottage was, by far, her favorite place. Homey and hidden behind a grove of tall trees, just outside the city limits, it hugged the hillside with the cityscape on one side, farms on the other, and the river flowing along its southern border.

Its gray stone walls always welcomed her from afar, and the view warmed her heart with expectation even before the fireplace inside was lit. A narrow, stony trail led toward the river where she and Pete—when they were younger—would play with rocks and build sand dunes on the beach.

In the evenings, their parents would build fires and roast

some meat or fish on it, if they caught one. Then they would set a blanket and enjoy the meal while their mom read them a book or their dad read a poem—usually his favorite poem —"O King".

Violet swiped another tear, but more great memories followed. She swallowed recalling her cottage bedroom's reading nook with its pirate lantern dangling from the edge. The nook had a wooden sword for a coat hanger and cozy red, white, and blue throw pillows coupled with a pink blanket.

Many summers were spent there devouring book after book and leaving a large pile at the foot of the bed. The best part of her day was when she'd later learn that her mom had ordered fresh book supplies at the local library and had swapped them for the finished pile.

Surprising herself with an unexpected chuckle, as a procession of the choir for a special presentation began, she recalled covering herself with a blanket to hide that she was reading a gripping tale, only to have her mom reach in and slip the book from beneath the covers and slap it closed with a thud—forcing Violet to sleep.

Christmas and New Year celebrations, usually spent at the cottage, were always memorable—until now. Considering that this was still early November, Thanksgiving and Christmas this year would be hard, *very hard*, to get through.

Last Christmas, even though her dad had been sick with what they had thought was pneumonia but turned out to be an issue with his lungs due to heavy smoking as a young man, he had insisted the three of them to go to the cottage to spend the holidays. Pete had accepted the invitation when she pressed on him how much their dad said he'd wanted to see his children together. But Pete warned that any praying would be without him. She'd agreed, excited to see their family under the same roof.

She'd spent time reading selected Scriptures from the book of Psalms and Proverbs, his favorite passages from the Bible, to their dad, who sat on a rocking chair in front of the fireplace. She smiled when she reached verses he liked. He would usually reward her with a smile, as well as mumble a repetition of the Scripture from memory or give other commentary while she continued reading out loud. Pete left them to it at some point and went fishing, though he returned hours later, having caught nothing.

At the end of Christmas Day after the reading was done, Dad had laid a gentle hand on her arm, then asked her to read his favorite poem, "O King". Even though she'd known he had been fond of that poem her whole life, at that moment in time, she realized the poem meant a lot to him.

And for that reason, she would ensure the poem's art still hanging prominently on the cottage wall was moved to her house. If nothing else, it would keep the memory alive. She remembered feeling somber that day as night fell, and they'd shared mugs of hot chocolate and marshmallows as she missed their mom. Clearly, they all missed her.

Then they'd watched some TV and prayed together when it got late, without Pete. That was the evening her dad officially gave over the reins of the company to Pete, signing all the paperwork, and handing them to his secretary who'd stopped by. He'd also named Violet to be in charge of the lab, as well as the ex-officio deputy to her brother. Though surprised at the move, she'd been fine with it since she still enjoyed her full-time job. She always suspected her dad may want her to move to work fully in his company someday, and she realized that the day was nearer than she'd wished for it to be.

Overall, that had been a better Christmas than she'd expected, better than they'd had for a long time. Not because they were completely taken with each other. No. But because they learned to love one another and accommodate each other's differences, without alienating anyone. They were a family once again, without prejudice. They knew each other's buttons and avoided pushing them. They gave without an expectation to receive.

Before going to bed then, they'd exchanged gifts. Pete had surprisingly bought Christmas gifts for them too—a blue sweater for their dad and a pair of pajamas for her, with a box of chocolate. More surprisingly, he'd recalled how much she loved her reindeer pajamas many Christmases ago and had bought her a pair. Which left her wondering...how much of the past did he remember? Did he recall his faith in Christ? She'd thanked him for the gift, but that spurred something else in her—a burden to pray. So, instead of wearing the pajamas, she took them and presented them to God in prayer on her knees.

Clearly, there was still some kindness left in Pete, a kindness she knew God could expand. She cried to Him to grow that patch of softness in Pete's heart until he repented and received Jesus afresh. She'd prayed for Pete long into that night, like her mom would typically do, then exhausted, she fell asleep.

An usher beckoned at her, and the wave drew Violet back to the service. But the elderly lady wasn't calling for her, but for her brother. So, she scooted to let him through. As Pete rose, he climbed to the altar. Soon, it would be her turn to speak.

As Pete stood there, he shared about who their dad meant to him, making it impossible not to see how much he resembled the senior Zendel. He spoke like him, paused in between sentences, and tilted his head when he was ruminating on his next words. "Dad was a very good man, a great father, and an admirable example to us."

Pete glanced toward Violet and swallowed hard. "He taught Vi and me how to hold our own and never back down in front of a challenge. He taught us that with hard work, and...God's help, we could achieve anything."

His gaze traveled to the urn, but she refused to follow it there. Then when he looked up again, his eyes were misty. "He always said today is more important than yesterday, so make sure to seize the day and don't waste it regretting what happened yesterday. Meaning, we should forget the past, optimize today, and plan for the future."

His Adam's apple bobbed. "Dad said to always do your best today because you are not guaranteed tomorrow. And if you get to see tomorrow, count yourself blessed and do it all over again."

He placed a hand on his chest. "I've held those words close to my heart as I learned to lead an organization he pioneered from the ground up. I've seen respect and admiration for him in the eyes of everyone whom I've met since taking up the duties of the CEO at Cortexe Corp."

She hardly heard his following words as her heart twisted with grief. Pete's voice, so much like their dad's, reminded her afresh that he was no longer here.

Violet jerked her head leftward moments later when someone called her name and beckoned her out to the aisle. Pete had finished speaking and returned toward their seat.

She drew in a deep breath, stood, walked past Pete, and then took the stage at the altar. As she stood there, she was grateful for the sheer number of people who had come to honor her dad. The church was full. She gripped both edges of the podium as her feet turned to jelly and her heart was melting with coming tears. She blinked and lost her struggle not to look at the urn. No. It couldn't be her dad in there. The gray oval sat unmoving, in contrast to the man he'd been.

Her eyes fastened to it, and she wanted to ask the urn to

give back her dad but knew it couldn't. Her eyes swam with tears, and someone stepped close and rubbed her back, though she didn't look to see who it was as she returned her gaze to the packed church watching her.

Violet glanced at Tim wearing a black suit seated behind the first row. When their eyes met, he nodded, giving her strength to continue. It had to be a sign, a gift from God, to give her strength on a tough day, while caught in a moment she wished she didn't have to go through. She inhaled another deep breath and cleared her throat.

Violet fixed her eyes to a point past their heads—and settled it on a cross affixed above the church entrance—as she spoke. She didn't allow herself to look at the urn again and undo the composure she was struggling to maintain. "Thank you all for coming to celebrate the life of our father. I appreciate your presence, your prayers, and your support.

"Losing him has been a hard blow." She sniffed past a tight throat. "Dad, our dad," she began, "was my hero. And I can't believe he's gone." Her voice broke. "He wasn't just Pete's and my dad." She waved to where she saw faces she'd recognized. "He was a dad to the youth church he pastored, whose members I see in the audience today." One of them nodded as her eyes met his. Through the corner of her eyes, she saw Tim rise, with a phone pressed to his ear, and step out the side door. She returned her focus to the service as someone started recording on video across from where she stood. She didn't mind as she'd seen how much effort the church had put in to support the funeral today. They must've hired the videographer.

"He was a father to his employees, his community, and as many of you have said to me, a mentor in this church." She bowed her head and prayed for grace to get through this. This was her eulogy of a man she honored and respected. She *would* get her words out. She *would* get through this.

"My best memories of him were at our family cottage where we often spent summers, Christmases, and New Years. He would roast marshmallows over an open fire at the private beach, and then read us a poem." She smiled painfully as the memories flooded her.

Her heart breaking, she lifted her head higher. "I could go on extolling him, but instead, I'll settle for sharing his favorite poem with you, a poem he said had been passed down from his dad. I'm not sure about its origin. Maybe it was something his dad wrote. I just know he'd read this to me from childhood, and I like it."

Her next words came effortlessly having heard and recited "O King" over and again throughout her lifetime. "The poem says:

Long may you live, O King!

Escape the Hunter when he comes

His heart is dark, his dagger is cloaked, and his finger is cut

He comes for Kings

And none see him coming

Escape the hunter every way you can

For the King is favored by God to live

Live among the orchards, vineyards, and garden of roses and blossom

Fresh as the air, sweet as the berries, and refreshing as the rain

Long may you live, O King!"

As she uttered the last words by heart, she allowed the following applause and the standing ovation to strengthen her for her walk back to her seat. "Adieu, Papa," she whispered.

Pete patted her arm as she reclaimed her seat. The rest of the funeral passed in a blur. But she felt comforted by all the friends and well-wishers who hugged her and followed them to the burial cemetery, and her heart broke even further as they buried him.

As far as she was concerned, her last safe place was gone, and only Jesus was truly her place of rest from now on.

She wrapped a hand around herself to ward off a chill as she entered the vehicle and headed to the lawyer's office for the will reading. There were no surprises. Her dad would want her to go to work for him at Cortexe Corp. alongside Pete, and his will indicated that. She chose to do so and to leave her teaching job at the college. She loved both equally, but preserving her dad's legacy through his company came out on top. By the time the lawyer was done, she felt drained.

This day—surely the longest day of her life—left her exhausted when she returned to the cottage with Pete. They ate some pizza in silence, grieving together, after which she said goodnight to Pete, who fielded business calls and responded to condolence callers.

With shoulders as heavy as ever, she went to her room, showered, changed her clothes, and slid beneath the covers. Battling sleep, she closed her eyes, thanked the Lord for gracing her through the funeral, and soon, she fell asleep.

10

"Do not marvel that I say to you, 'You must be born again.'"
–John 3:7

~

Angel woke up with a sharp pain shooting across her midsection. She groaned, sucked in her breath, and blinked behind heavy eyelids. As the smell of disinfectants hit her nostrils, she was sure of one thing—she was in a hospital. She tried to move but couldn't. Unable to recall how she got here, she pressed a hand to her forehead.

How long had she been out? If the signatures and get-well-soon wishes written all around her cast were anything to go by, she must've been out for more than one day. Some were dated Monday, one Tuesday, and another Wednesday. She eased away the oxygen mask blocking her view of her body. As she struggled to lift herself to rise, more pain shot up her legs, and she groaned and settled back down.

Then she saw she wasn't alone.

"Stephanie? John?" Her siblings sat flanking the bed, each holding onto the bedside railing. Were they...*praying*? Maybe Stephanie, but certainly not John.

Just then, the door opened. Her partner shuffled in with a slower stride, probably due to his injuries during the attack at his home.

Her little sister, Stephanie, covered her face, sobbing quietly.

Angel turned her glance to John, who was muttering... something. A prayer? Quite unlikely.

At her words, his head lifted. Then he drew closer, eyes rounded. "Oh, you're awake. I was worried." Concern lined his thick brow. "I got home from the fellowship I attended with Tim. Then I went to the store to buy some milk when the call came. They said you'd been shot and were in surgery."

He rubbed his brow. "So I called Stephanie and the others. We waited until you were out of surgery. Hughes and Grace will be back in an hour."

John then bowed his head and raised it. "You scared me. And I prayed for the first time. I prayed so you won't die. And," he gulped, "I wasn't sure God would hear someone like me. But I'm glad He answered. I didn't expect that." The room grew quiet, and, unable to speak past a tight throat, she squeezed his hand when it settled in hers. "I may reconsider my rejection of Christ after all."

Was she hearing correctly? After all these years of praying and hoping for him to accept Christ and giving up hope were they truly one step closer? "So, you'll go to fellowship again?"

"Yes." A lone tear rolled down his cheek. John was never the type to shed tears. Whatever happened must've shaken him. "They said you coded twice, Angel. I'll go to church again. If only to go and thank God for saving my big sister's life. I appreciated your worth when I woke up and you weren't there. I've... taken you for granted." His voice broke. "I knew I had to have a chance to apologize. I'm going to clean up my act, arrange to settle my debt, then get my life together. For good this time."

"I'd applaud you for that choice, young man." Her partner, Pierce, stepped forward. "It's better doing it with Jesus, John. I know these are the things you want to do, but I also know from experience, that the road to getting those things accomplished successfully, and without any more regrets, passes through Jesus."

"I appreciate your words." John nodded. "Like I said, I'm willing to give Jesus a try."

"Fair enough." Her partner turned to her, and his smile

seemed to lift the pain pinching his eyes. "And it's good to see the sleeping beauty is now awake. You scared us all. What were you thinking landing into a dangerous place alone like that?"

"Justice..." Angel managed before her throat tightened again, still reeling over the news—She'd coded? And John was getting serious with Jesus? She adjusted her pillow to lean up slightly. Could she dare to be hopeful for him after virtually giving up?

"Lady Justice, you need to stay alive to execute justice, too, so no more taking excessive risks." He wagged a reproving finger. "Next time, you wait for me or someone else before going to interview a suspect. We never know when things might turn ugly. Are we agreed?"

Angel grunted her disagreement, and they all laughed, except her. She wanted the criminals caught, not waiting to pet them into talking. Granted, she'd taken a risk, but it had paid off with the information.

The weakness making her drowsy again, she slid down the pillow. "Thank you all." She would need a couple of weeks to heal. But she would get back on those criminals' trail. Then, as sleep shuttered her eyes, she muttered, "Soon."

VIOLET TOOK THREE WEEKS SORTING THROUGH THEIR PARENTS'

belongings before finally getting comfortable enough to resume her full-time duties at Cortexe Corp.

She found a few surprises. Like a golden heart locket bequeathed to her by her parents and which she now wore everywhere. Plus, they'd left the cottage to her, while Pete inherited their family home. Then they left her a key. She wasn't sure where it fitted into or what it was for, and so had a jeweler unseal the locket, insert the little key, then seal it again since she wore the locket everywhere. Hopefully, one day, she'd figure out what the key was for.

Still missing her dad, she grieved his loss, but she'd admonished herself that sitting indoors and crying wouldn't bring him back. So she tried to resume her life, starting with Cortexe Corp., which was running smoothly under her brother's leadership. For the past year, she'd been working at the Cortexe Corp. lab with the technicians while unofficially functioning as the Deputy CEO, who had retired the previous year. She had a management office on the top floor next to Pete's, but enjoyed her hands-on lab work. A day-to-day chief scientist managed the staff there, but she oversaw their work when needed. She also supplied whatever the technicians and staff requested.

Pete had an undeniable knack for leadership. But working with him for the past year, while teaching at the college showed he also had an aggressive ambition that had to be monitored. She hoped to help him balance both sides of his personality without clashing as often as they recently had in private. Since the funeral, things had been calm, but she couldn't assume they would remain so.

Upon arriving at the complex, she stepped out of her white sedan and, while walking toward the towering complex, uttered a quick prayer for her first full day to go smoothly, especially with Pete. She strode past the familiar Cortexe Corp. inscription on white marble and entered the expansive lobby.

A life-sized banner image of Pete smiling greeted her. Standing at the entrance and with her eyes shielded by large dark sunglasses, she halted her stride, inhaled the pine-scented air-freshening fragrance, and released her breath with a single word, "Interesting." He was sure putting his stamp on the company. But was this new addition his idea or did someone suggest it?

Sometimes, it struck her, like right now, how much they looked alike. Of course, she chose to wear large sunglasses today to avoid the stares she'd get without them. Her nerves were wound up enough already.

"Miss Zendel?" She spun to a security guard approaching with cautious steps, one hand idling on his weapon.

She raised her hand and took off the glasses. "Yes."

He closed the distance and shook her hand, and his shoulders dropped upon recognition. "This way, please. Your security escorts will be waiting at the elevator. Both of them." He ushered her forward. Then they took a turn, and two broad-chested men fixed their gazes on her.

She swallowed. She had bodyguards? A driver had been enough. And even then, she'd asked to drive herself in for a few days to have privacy to pray during her commute.

When she reached them, she paused, and they greeted her with a wave and a small smile. Then one held the elevator for her while the security guard returned to his duty post. She managed to stop herself from smiling when she saw the numbers on the elevator buttons were now math symbols not digits. Another change Pete had made, but this one she liked. When they were kids and had visited their dad's office, Pete said he'd do it. She hadn't realized it had meant so much to him then.

The elevator doors closed and, after a soft bounce, carried them up to a secure floor. As soon as they exited, Pete was standing there.

"Welcome, Vi. Glad to see you here." A quick hug followed.

"Thanks." She returned his hug.

His gaze dropped to her neck. "You got the locket." He said it as a statement of fact.

"Yes. I didn't know about it, but Dad and Mom apparently left it to me. I found it with a note addressed to me in their bedroom drawer. You knew about it?"

Pete nodded. "I saw it years back and had asked Dad for it. He said it was for those in the family who followed The Way. I guess I didn't qualify."

"Oh." The Way meaning Jesus. Was this that important?

"I didn't realize. I'm sorry?"

Pete shrugged. "Hey, it's their choice and I respect it. I'm glad you got it at least."

He stepped aside and pointed forward. "This way, please."

Her bodyguards-cum-security-escorts trailed his bodyguards as he led her down a long stretch of offices, introducing her to the COO, among others. She smiled and managed to hold onto as many names as she could. But she'd need more interaction to know them at a glance. As they passed office after office, almost all the staff members, who had worked closely under their dad's leadership, were gone. Did Pete fire them or did they leave on their own? Some worry crept up her spine. She would find a chance to ask Pete why he made all the physical and managerial changes—and perhaps, what other changes were coming in order to better support him.

Their leadership styles were different and could prompt a mass exodus of people who preferred their dad's family-style work atmosphere to Pete's formality. But she hoped Pete would retain some sense of community so the oldcomers wouldn't feel estranged.

Her phone rang inside her purse, and she paused and picked up the call. "Hello?"

Heavy breathing followed.

When a clicking met her ear, Violet curved her brows and moved the phone away to look at the screen. She blinked at the white words against a black background. "TELL ME ABOUT THE POEM." Then the call disconnected.

Pete walked back to her. "Vi? Are you all right?"

Raising her glance to him, she wasn't sure how to explain what had happened as the words, like grainy sand, cleared off her phone. "Someone called me, and instead of talking, typed out a question asking about a poem."

"Dad's poem?" His brows inched up. When she nodded, he frowned. "Why would anyone care about an old poem?" He reached out and took her phone, handing it to one of her bodyguards. "Take this to the lab and investigate who the message was from." While the man left with her phone, Pete ushered her forward, appearing to be more intent on getting started with their day than in dealing with her caller. But she'd been rattled.

"The bigger question is how does he know about dad's poem?" How much could the team find out? There'd been no voice to analyze. The call barely lasted ten seconds and came from an unregistered number. But she relented, not inter- ested in arguing with Pete. "Could it be as a result of my pres- ence here? Did someone object to my working here as Deputy CEO? Or was there a disgruntled employee since the call came in now while I'm here?" But why would someone be against her role in her dad's company?

Pete gave her a bland look. "Really, Vi?"

"Sorry, but I have to ask." She pushed back. "I take my safety seriously."

"As do I," he replied. Some silence followed. Then he led them forward again. This wasn't how she wanted things to start.

"Fine. Let me know what they find out."

His nod ended the conversation, and she trailed him to his office for their first official meeting. But something told her things would only go downhill from there.

11

"Nor is there salvation in any other, for there is no other name under heaven given among men by which we must be saved." –Acts 4:12

∼

"I got the job," John's announcement helped Angel through the final round of her physical therapy for the day. She climbed down from the machine and hugged her brother, sure that he wouldn't mind a sweaty hug. Angel was so thankful that every day she felt stronger and stronger. Beyond the occasional pain and scarring, she scarcely suffered lasting injuries.

"That is the best news yet I've heard today. Congratulations!" She held him at an arm's length and wished words could describe how much he'd changed—and how happy that made her. In the weeks since he'd returned, she'd seen him mature, both physically and spiritually.

He'd become more patient, attended fellowship with Tim every week this month, and was going again next week. She found him spending time early in the morning studying his Bible and praying. That was new—and pleasant to see. She prayed harder in her heart for him to come to salvation in Christ, and with the way things were going, it seemed that would only be a matter of time.

It was not a secret that John had ruined his life. But it was also not a secret that God was turning things around for the better for him. Getting this new job being the latest in that trend. The restoration of his relationship with their younger sister, Stephanie, being the first. Stephanie had found it hard to forgive him for cutting off from them, and they'd had issues for a decade. She had been angry over the way John had been living his life. But, in recent weeks, they'd grown close, arriving at the hospital together, going out for lunch, and him saying amen when Stephanie prayed before they left Angel at the hospital. This new family that God gifted her was so good that it left Angel speechless most times. She just watched the miracles unfolding and thanked God.

"Thank you." John supported her with a hand as she knelt to get her pearl earring that had fallen during her exercise.

When she straightened, the hospital therapist gave her a thumbs-up. "Now, you're in such good shape, and you're about ready to go home. But after you're discharged tomorrow, I suggest you rest for an extra two weeks before returning to strenuous work. I will recommend that to your doctors."

Knowing she was getting discharged had also been a blessing. "Thank you. But can I work from home?"

Her therapist nodded. "As long as you follow the exercise and therapy and rest regimen, you should be fine." She moved toward the exit. "I'll see you for a checkup in three weeks."

Eager to leave the hospital setting and not step foot in one again as a patient for a long time, she was definitely grateful for the freedom to go home. She spun to John, who was collecting her items—sneakers and her purse for her for transport back to her room—while she grabbed the sweaty face towels and switched from sneakers to flat boots. "When do you start the job?"

"I let them know I'm available now, and that works for them. So, I'll be starting tomorrow. But I'll be home to check on you around one p.m. I'm a site supervisor, so I won't do the hands-on work but rather ensure things are running smoothly." John led the way toward the exit.

～

IT TOOK TWO WEEKS AND THREE REMINDERS FOR THE SECURITY team to get back to Violet about the strange call. By then, she had settled into her duties and mastered the art of avoiding conflict with Pete. They'd clashed on company issues twice, once in the presence of others, and she wouldn't allow a repeat.

But Pete was changing fast, thanks to his growing friendship with the newly hired COO. Apparently, the guy had been hired just before their dad handed things over to Pete a year ago, but he had played a minor role in primary decision making until now. And he considered her an enemy.

She wasn't about to allow some criminally-minded fellow ruin her parents' company. So she stood up to them both— like right now with both men in her office convincing her of a need to purchase additional security and hire more manpower. "Guys," she folded her hands on the smooth-polished mahogany desk before her—her dad's desk—and drew a deep breath, taking comfort from the connection to him, "if what we're trying to achieve is to restructure the company, I'm all for it. But starting an internship, building a campus here, and paying for more software is currently outside our budget and our scope of operations. Why do we need to do all that?"

"Expansion." Pete slid into the chair in her office while his bodyguards hovered beyond the glass doors. "We have to expand. The world is moving forward, and we need to move ahead of the curve. We need to take on progressive projects, and I have just the idea for that. One scientist at the lab has been working on it for some time now."

He spread out his arms wide. "But I want it bigger. We can only attract heftier investment when we go big. I know a contact who works with foreign investors, and I gave him a call. He has interested parties standing by. He's simply waiting for our go-ahead."

When she shook her head, Pete leaned forward. "Vi, this is our chance. We seize it or we miss it. I have to build on what Dad did here. The security industry needs more eyes in the sky. I will provide them with the equipment by leveraging what already exists and connecting them all. That is why I commissioned The Rulebook, which the tech team is working on. But we need more money for the project to continue, and there are investors willing to finance us."

Violet also leaned forward, palms down now on Dad's desk, the strength of the man who had sat there for decades seemingly holding her up. "Do you know about the possibility of possession of any criminal records by your potential investors? Granted, I spend all my time at the lab, but I also care what decisions you make up here. If you need me to step in and be the voice of caution, I will."

Crossing his legs, Pete narrowed his gaze at the COO. "He'd said you wouldn't listen. And I wished he was wrong. I wanted us to do this together, but it appears I need to go it alone." Some desperation cooled his tone and sent caution racing up her spine.

"Pete, do you know the identities of these investors?" But he was silent, as though his mind was made up. He was going with the COO on this, against her wishes.

That caution shivered deeper into her heart. Feeling double-crossed, she still spoke her mind without fear. "The company is not in trouble. We're not strapped for cash and looking for investors. We're fine. If we keep doing what we're doing, we can expand slowly. This Rulebook project sounds dicey to me, and there are no guarantees of success. If I were you, I'd tread carefully."

Even as a kid, Pete disliked anyone standing up to him, so she took a risk. She had quit her professorial job, so her full-time income now came from Cortexe Corp. But she fought for her parents' legacy. They had sown all they had into this company, truly grown it from the ground up, and she wouldn't allow Pete to mortgage all that on a scientific experiment with possible criminals.

"Either you come along or you don't." Pete rose and approached the door. At her voice, he paused.

"I think I'll prefer to spend more time down at the lab. I'd rather not be in your way since your mind was made up before you came asking." She pressed palms deep against the desk, sadness achingly echoing in the finality of her words. "Oh, and please keep your bodyguards. I'm sure I can navigate this building by myself."

He squeezed the door open without looking back. "Suits me fine." The COO led the way. Pete followed, and as soon as the door closed, Violet didn't have to ask. Battle lines reverberated through their exchanged words and left little room for dialogue. Was this truly the beginning of the end for their peaceful collaboration? "I'm sorry, Dad," she whispered.

Her phone rang, and she picked up the call. "Hello?"

A clicky sound followed, and she jerked the phone back from her ear.

"I WANT TO KNOW ABOUT THE POEM." The call ended like it had the first time, and she slid the phone into her purse, rose, and headed down to the lab, determined. She was a computer analyst and wouldn't wait for someone else to find out who was bothering her. Then she called the police to report the incident, also informing them about the first one. She was done waiting for Pete. And done trusting him with her safety. He was uncontrollable.

12

"...Make known what are the riches of the glory of this mystery among the Gentiles: which is Christ in you, the hope of glory." —Colossians 1:27

~

Angel arrived at work two weeks after leaving the hospital, to a rousing round of applause, a cluster of balloons dancing over her desk, and a warm welcome. Hugs, followed by appreciation for the risk she had taken, were given by her colleagues, and she couldn't feel any more loved and appreciated. Or more ready to dive into her case afresh.

As soon as she settled into her seat, her cellphone rang. She frowned at it. It was a bit early to be getting a call. "Hello?"

"Hi, Angel?" a vaguely familiar voice asked.

"Yes. Who is this?"

"Tim Santiago. Do you have a moment to chat? I promise it won't take long. But you'll want to know about this."

She swallowed hard. "Sure. What's up?" Tim had become like second family since he and John became friends. He'd progressed from a spiritual coach for her brother, to a life coach, and now a trusted friend. His positive impact had altered their family for good, and she had expressed her gratitude to him several times.

"Actually, I think you may want to be a part of this."

Her curiosity piqued, she batted a yellow balloon aside and used a paperweight to pin its curly ribbon further away. "Um, part of what?"

"John's water baptism. He received Jesus in the early hours of this morning after we'd talked for almost two hours. He called me around three a.m. And I suspect the only reason you haven't heard is that he might be asleep."

Angel sunk into her chair, a gray balloon floated skyward, and tears pooled in her eyes. "Are you kidding me?" A happy sob escaped her lips.

"No, I'm serious. Congratulations. He had a lot of questions, and I walked him through the answers I knew from Scripture. I was thrilled when, as we wrapped up, he said he wished to receive Jesus. So I led him in confessing the Sinner's Prayer. Mission accomplished. John is now a part of the family of Jesus."

Tears warmed tracks down her cheeks as she waved off Pierce's concern over her crying. "I'm so happy. You just made my year. Thank you for sharing this news. And yes, I will come for his baptism. Seven p.m. is the usual time, right?"

"Yes, it is. The pastor is taking care of this one."

"Thank you for everything, Tim. Really, thank you. Heaven knows how grateful I am and will repay you for this labor of love."

"My pleasure, Angel. But remember, it is the Lord who uses us to accomplish His divine purpose, not us. I am only a vessel."

"A willing vessel. That made a huge difference."

Static joined Tim's chuckle. "Well, you're right about the big difference we've seen in John. I'm also glad to hear you're feeling better. Stay safe out there."

"See you later, Tim. And...thanks again."

As she hung up, Angel was sure her day and life had just gotten brighter. She smiled at the bright yellow balloon, dancing between her monitor and her stacked desktop file tray, feeling herself to be just as cheery and light weight. If anyone asked her, this was as close to the best day of her life as she could imagine. John was saved. She hummed "Amazing Grace" as she powered on her PC. *Thank You, Lord Jesus. You did it for me.*

∾

VIOLET ALIGHTED FROM HER CAR AT THE CORTEXE CORP. complex with heavy steps. She and Pete had just had their worst argument over the phone last night. How could she even come into work today? But they had a scheduled meeting she couldn't afford to miss. Weeks upon weeks of her hard work dangled in-between Pete's ambition and the company's wellbeing.

Massaging her forehead to ease the dull ache with one hand, she felt for her purse in the front passenger seat. If she chose to go through this day with her brother, taking a pain reliever would be a must. She rummaged through her purse, found some Aleve, and drank two. Then she returned the remainder of her bottled water to the cup-holder, stepped out, and slung the purse over her shoulder. At the door, she spun around. She hadn't locked the car. She sighed and shook her head, choosing not to return to lock it. It should be fine within the complex with the heavy security.

She clutched her purse, pushed through the doors with weary feet, thanks to a sleepless night, and paused to check the time. She smiled—7:44 a.m. She had fifteen minutes to settle into her office, put her purse down, and then head to the meeting.

As soon as she stepped past the rotating lobby doors, she froze. Pete stood there looking directly at her, with one hand shoved into the pocket of his black pants. He'd dyed his hair a strange color somewhere between golden brown and milky white.

He was a different person from who she'd left here the previous day. Ignoring the hair color, for now, she closed the distance between them and stopped within a handshake's distance. Anger swirled around him, and with his lips pinched white, he must be working hard to contain his fury.

But she wouldn't give in to whatever his demands might be—if that was why he stood here. She hitched her purse higher on her shoulder and arched her chin, trying not to think about how perfectly matched their heights were when so little else now seemed the same. "Why are you waiting for me here? Our meeting is at eight."

The COO emerged from behind him, so there had to be trouble. Without acknowledging him, she didn't let her gaze waver, holding Pete's eye to eye unflinching.

The COO cleared his throat, and peripheral vision revealed an evil grin as it twitched his dark mustache. "That would be my fault. I should've called you to give you a heads-up." He slid a hand into his pocket and winked. "Oops."

Her frown deepened, pinching her own lips to match Pete's. "A heads-up to me about what?"

"We're restricting your building access." Pete moved closer. "You will be granted full access to the general entrances and exits, as well as the lab. But no more than that."

She crossed her arms. "Since when? Remember, I also have authority in this company. You cannot make unilateral decisions as you choose."

He turned, and the bodyguards advanced before he took a step. "If you violate these conditions, disciplinary actions will follow, up to and including termination. Are we clear?" Of course, he turned his back to her. He couldn't say that to her face. But his bodyguards? Fear laced their eyes for her brother. And her heart constricted with a similar yet stronger fear, for him, not about him. Did he become so obsessed with power and control that he forgot to be good-natured?

She strode around the guards to stand face to face with him, eye to eye once again. "Dare you say that to my face, Pete? You might have the executive authority, but I can petition to take over the company if you're going in the wrong direction."

Something blazed in his eyes, making her wish for his previous coolness. Lurching forward, he stood inches from her face. "Only if I'm incapacitated, and I'm not. You lack the legal grounds for such. And I will fight you. Are you ready to get into a stinking fight because this will be ugly?"

Pete knew she loved him and would hesitate to engage in a public spar.

He guessed as much with her frustrated silence. "Sorry, sis. I remain in charge. And you don't dare flout my rules around here or you face the consequences." He stormed off, leaving everyone in the lobby quiet at the altercation.

So, she squared her shoulders and marched to the lab. There, she asked about the lead scientist who worked on The Rulebook. Something was going on.

"The roster was edited to say he was on leave this week," an assistant informed her.

"Thank you." She massaged her neck as she entered her office and sat. Her office at the lab was much smaller, but more peaceful, though, in this moment, she would have loved to touch her father's desk, envision him sitting there, guiding the company. If only Pete had cared to take that desk. Would memories of the man behind it have tempered him?

Shaking her head, she got to work on the tasks she had set up for the day and refused to think about Pete. Anything she did now would be out of anger, and she wasn't going to react like that.

Around lunchtime, her phone rang. She smiled at Tim's contact. "Hey."

"Hi, Violet. How's your day going?"

She wondered whether to answer in a formal respectful manner or to share her problems. But this was Tim. "To be honest, Tim, I could use a friend right about now."

Tim huffed a sigh. "It's Pete again, isn't it?"

"Yes."

"If you want to talk, I'm a friendly ear. Hey, can we do lunch? Right now? There's this restaurant, La Mesa De Comedore, not far from you there. Can we meet up in say, one hour?"

"Sure. I haven't eaten, and my belly is growling. I know where it is, and I'll see you then." As she hung up the call, she prayed for grace to get through her day without further bad occurrences.

~

INHALING AN APPEASING BREATH, VIOLET ALLOWED THE SAVORY dishes before her to soothe away some of her worry.

"What happened?" Seated at the La Mesa De Comedore, Tim forked some roasted corn and some mayo as well as chicken to his plate from the large dish they'd ordered.

Violet followed suit to serve herself. And as soon as she'd taken a bite, she sat back to figure out how to shape her response politely. "I don't know what Pete is doing. And I think he wants to force me out."

"Out of the company? That's impossible." His eyes narrowed. "Right? I mean, the will stated that you both have ownership stakes in it as the only surviving children."

She offered a brief nod and sipped some water to douse the hotness of the soup. "Yes, but Pete has the executive authority. I'm more involved in the lab, and I only take over if he is deemed incapacitated."

"Well, he's not sick so..." Tim swallowed, and a dark line tightened his brow. "But with Pete being the way he is, that's not good either. I don't think your parents foresaw this. What are you going to do?"

She let her spoon sink deep into the chicken tortilla soup but didn't immediately lift it, swirling vegetables and black beans into a whirl. "If it was someone else, it would've been easier." She swallowed her food and shook her head. "What can I do, huh? He's my brother, and as much as I don't want to see him ruin everything, there is nothing apparently wrong. If I took this to court, nothing could prove the company is being jeopardized, beyond my gut feeling."

"And Pete's animosity. Don't forget that." Tim set his fork down. "And stripping of some of your authority."

"Right, those too." Violet ate some more as Tim picked up his fork and ate in silence. "Again, I'm trying to avoid a public spar. It will jeopardize future investment prospects. I'm stuck between tough choices. I want to hold out hope for my brother, and I choose to relinquish any power he wants. After all, I have more than enough to meet my needs."

"This is plain wrong. Vi, let me know if there is anything I can do. You can always go back to teaching." He toyed with the edge of his napkin. "It's an alternative."

"Yes. But...well, something about seeing the only family member you have left heading toward ruin and taking everything else down with him makes you not want to let that happen, even if you can't stop it." The words, a whisper, seemed to strain through her closed throat. Why was she even trying to eat?

"Maybe you should both talk to a professional. A mediator might bridge the gap."

Violet choked a laugh. "Does Pete seem agreeable to a mediator to you? He is in charge, remember?" She edged the bowl away. She couldn't stomach another spoonful. "I think I lost my appetite."

"If you're going to face Pete, you need to eat. I have an idea of something you can do."

A spark of curiosity, and faint hope, shot through her. She scooted forward, studying him for a clue. "Okay. Tell me."

He winked. "Only after you finish eating, so eat up."

Sighing, she picked up her spoon and ate some more.

"So, you say you were getting strange messages. Have the cops identified a culprit? Did they find anything? Or did you?" Tim asked as he too rounded off the meal with a belch a little louder than he probably would've liked. "Sorry about that."

That led her to chuckle. "No apologies, it's a natural phenomenon."

They both laughed. "Just like Professor Ben used to say."

The memory calmed her a bit. "Actually, I didn't find anything. The number was a dead end, and the cops haven't seen anything to flag. So, there's nothing. They blamed it on a possible sick prankster taking advantage of my dad's passing."

"Sick prankster indeed." Tim sipped some water, wiped his mouth with the napkin, then sat back too. "But don't you find it weird that a prankster, however sick, would resort to hiding his identity, risking police trouble, and doing it twice just for a prank? I'm not sure I accept that version."

He sat up as she finished eating and pushed her plate aside, sure that she couldn't consume another morsel. "That's where my suggestion can come in handy in identifying this culprit too. You hear me out, then choose what to do."

"I'm listening, Tim." She prayed that whatever he suggested she could legitimately do. Sure, Tim was a Christian, but she had to keep her own conscience clear in whatever she put her hands into. "It's just...with my and Pete's emotions being so raw after our dad's death, grief could partly account for his recent behavior. It might not be, but I want us to keep that in mind. He could also be trying to establish himself, although I deem it unnecessary. I'm not excusing him, but I wanted us to keep all the relevant pieces in perspective."

"And that's why I'm suggesting you play along until you find out what this is all about."

"Ooookay." Violet tapped a finger on her water glass, unsure how to react. "Go on."

Tim leaned over the table. "Look at it this way. If Pete is involved in something wrong, or if this Rulebook thing is worth pursuing, how would you know from the outside? You can only know if you're still inside the company, working with him. Moreover, you might also utilize the lab facilities to discover who your mystery caller is." He rolled up his sleeve and paused. "I'm sure you love your brother, but the same cannot be said of him, unfortunately. You don't have to take my word, but based on what you've shared, I don't see any other viable options for what you want to have happen. So, I've got a second piece of advice for you."

"Sure. What is it?"

"Get a journal. Write everything down. Everything you do from here on forward." He shrugged. "Including how this whole situation makes you feel. You know, write it down, especially if you can't tell anyone about it. So that tomorrow, you can find the strength to face what comes next. You won't be able to do that if you bottle it all up inside. And thirdly, pray. Pray like you've never prayed before, Vi. This is a storm of life. And no storm comes without a mission. But prayer turns those waves around to work for you, instead of against you. I'll be praying for you too. You can be sure of that."

Violet appreciated her friend's advice, knowing it came from a perfect heart, full of only concern for her. She settled a hand on his arm. "Thank you. I love everything you've said and will keep it in mind."

She closed her eyes, trying to envision how to handle this better than he'd suggested. Unable to find other suitable alternatives, she popped her eyelids open as BREAKING NEWS came on the air. Tim seemed ready to say something, but he turned to the wall-mounted TV as well.

"We interrupt your scheduled programming to inform you that a body found at a construction site downtown has been identified as this man." An image flashed on the screen, and she blinked at the TV, then swallowed hard. It was the Cortexe Corp. scientist supposedly on leave.

13

"For there is nothing hidden which will not be revealed, nor has anything been kept secret but that it should come to light."
–Mark 4:22

~

"Tim," Violet's ears tingled, and she rasped. "He was said to be on leave. He's...*dead*?" She clutched her chest, gasping.

"You know him?"

She pressed her fist harder against her chest. "He's the lead analyst for The Rulebook, and I was told he was on leave for one week. He had argued with Pete on Friday. I didn't get involved, and I wasn't listening. I had my earbuds on. I figured they'd work whatever it was out."

She and Tim stared at each other, pondering, knowing, wishing they weren't thinking it. But one of them had to say the words.

Violet braved it. "You think," she gulped, "do you think Pete had something to do with it? I'm scared, Tim. If he did this..." She ran a hand through her hair. "This isn't who he was. This isn't my brother." Words failed her. "I don't know who Pete Zendel is anymore."

He touched her hand and held his there until she met his gaze. "Don't make any assumptions yet. Ask him, hear him out, then make choices. I hate how this looks, but please," his eyes bore into hers with seriousness, "I know Pete has contacts with the police, but find a cop you can trust and tell him everything. My police friend would've been perfect, but she just survived a shooting and is dealing with some family issues. I would hesitate to expose her to anything potentially dangerous so soon. Considering this new development, it is even more important to write everything down now. Make sure you document as much as you can."

He paused like he was thinking and sucked in his lower lip. "I'm not sure it's wise for you to quit now even if you were thinking about doing so. Since you were at the same lab as the deceased guy, if you leave now, it will seem suspicious. Moreover, with this guy out of the picture, Pete will likely rely on you for the completion of this project."

"If he asks for me to take over, what do I do then?" Everything was happening so fast the room spun and developments left her with no space to think. Since Tim wasn't directly involved, surely, he had a clearer perspective which she could count on.

"There are two options. You walk away—he succeeds in securing someone willing to create something that threatens the world instead of protecting it. Or you stay and destroy it. If he offers you the chance, I'd say, you should accept it. But if it turns evil, you make sure you take the program down— unfailingly. Don't be responsible for a catastrophe, Vi. Everything is now on your shoulders. And I'm sorry you've found yourself in this unenviable situation."

He cast a glance at the TV again. "And if Pete did this, then he's covered his tracks pretty well. The problem we're facing now is this—if he killed once, he'll do it again. Don't be a victim. Be careful and get out if you feel unsafe."

She nodded and squeezed his hand. "I will."

"Promise me," he pressed.

"I promise."

He leaned back, then drew a long breath. "Good. Because while I'm away for a year, I need to be sure you'll be okay."

"Wait." Violet blinked. "Where are you going to?"

"I wish I knew all of this was going on before I took the position of adjunct faculty at the Department of Archeology in the University of Mexico." He sighed. "I can't cancel it now."

"Oh no, don't cancel it. We both knew you wanted this. But what a great surprise. Congratulations. I'm glad we came for lunch this afternoon then." She smiled. "I'm going to miss you." She tapped on his chest with a finger. "Don't go wandering into museums and getting shot at. You be careful too."

His laughter rang out so normal—and sounded like sweet music to her ears. It had been long since she heard those sounds. At least, she had something to smile about, even if only for a moment. And she was sure going to miss Tim. "Text me your email address, your phone number there, and your mailing address. Every form of communication possible. Skyping, whatever works."

"Of course, I will." He folded the napkin and set it beside his plate. "There is someone I led to Christ last night, or shall we say, early this morning. I'm heading to church tonight for his baptism."

"Oh, that sure makes me glad to hear. Congrats on that too. Unfortunately, Pete is far from the possibility of such an occasion happening for him."

"Don't give up, Vi. God can work a miracle tomorrow. In fact, He will, at His time. Keep praying and thanking Him in advance."

Nodding, she gave what she was sure was a sad smile. "When do you leave for your assignment?"

"In two weeks. Just enough time to know you're okay around Pete before I get on the plane."

"Thank you." Tim was looking out for her like her

brother should, like Pete should. Tim paid for their meal, and they rose to leave.

As soon as they exited the restaurant, her phone rang. It was Pete. Since the day he called her to tell her about the loss of their dad, she dreaded picking up his calls, suspecting he called when something was wrong.

With recent developments, she needed time to think before talking to him, so she let the call go to voicemail. At the valet parking, while she waited for her car to be brought to the front, she listened to the message. "Vi, it's Pete. Please come back to the office. We need to talk."

That was it?

She sighed and hugged Tim. "Thank you for lunch. And...for your advice. I appreciate it."

"Remember everything I said." He held her gaze, waiting.

A slight nod dipped her chin. "I will. You keep me posted about your plans."

"Will do. Bye for now, Vi." He shrugged his coat tighter to ward off the slight chill.

"Bye, Tim." As she watched him drive away, she felt like she lost her only friend and remaining family in the same day. Tim was more than a friend—he was a brother, a brother in Christ. She prayed she wouldn't have any emergency that would make him cancel his trip. It meant too much to him. Then she entered her car and drove off, en route to Cortexe Corp.

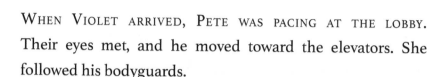

WHEN VIOLET ARRIVED, PETE WAS PACING AT THE LOBBY. Their eyes met, and he moved toward the elevators. She followed his bodyguards.

He marched forward, pushed the button, and while they waited, confusion and caution warred in her heart. So, she prayed. *Lord Jesus, I'm not sure how to handle whatever Pete is about to throw at me. But give me grace, wisdom, and direction in Jesus' name.*

The elevator pinged, and one by one, they all filed in. Then the doors sealed them in oppressive silence. But she was tired of avoiding confrontations while his choices degenerated from bad to worse. It was time they had at it, and whatever came out of this situation, God would take control.

She added a few more words to the prayer. *Lord, I know how much he hates to see or even hear about Jesus. It's almost like a taboo. He's my only family left, and while I can tiptoe around him to keep a semblance of a relationship, this time calls for being explicit with Your permission. Please, help me.*

The elevator chimed again at the executive floors. Pete led them toward his office, and her eyeballs rounded at the sheer size of the team working upstairs now on this project. So, Pete had hired the new employees and scaled up The Rulebook projected timeline—judging from the wall timer—all without telling her? What more was happening that she didn't know?

They walked into his office, and by then, she felt like her heart would burst. Staying calm was a struggle.

"Please, have a seat." He pointed to a swivel chair.

She shook her head. "I won't need a seat for this." She turned to his bodyguards. "Please excuse us. I need to speak with my brother alone. Now."

They stayed rooted, glancing at Pete, but he said nothing.

A fire rose from the pit of her belly and burst out of her lips. She reached out and flung the door open. "Get out! Now!" she roared. Without waiting for Pete, they marched out, and she kicked the door shut with a resounding thud. She spun, curled her arms, and faced Pete again, after adjusting her pinstriped suit.

Pete shrank back with a step. "Wow. That, I have never seen from you. Well, I guess we have all changed, haven't we?"

"Actions and reactions are equal and opposite, scientists say." She pressed her lips tightly and looked Pete in the eye, a mirror of hers. "And no, we haven't all changed for the worse." She pointed at him. "But you have."

She leaned forward and pinned both hands on the glistening glass desk. "I want you to tell me what you did to that dead young man. Something tells me you had a hand in his demise. I know you are capable of a lot of things, but killing an innocent man wasn't one of them. Yet. Tell me that hasn't changed."

Pete spun and walked off to a cabinet, uncorked a bottle

of wine and poured it over ice. He took the glass, returned to his desk, and took a sip. Then he gulped half the glass, set it down, and laughed. "You know, Vi, you might be my sister, but there are things you never ask a man. Who he sleeps with and how he makes his money."

She held his gaze with her steady one. "I didn't ask you any of those questions. The truth never hides from discovery forever, no matter how long you conceal it. Now, you tell me what role you might have played in that young man's demise or I'm going to the cops. And if you did anything complicit, I will go to the cops anyway."

That jerked his eyes into a frown. "You want to call the cops on me?" He came around his desk and loomed a breath away. "How dare you!" he drawled. "Try that, and I'll rend you before nightfall."

"You don't scare me, *mi querido hermano.* I'll call them *only* if you're guilty, Pete." She remained unflinching as his alcoholic breath poured on her face. "So, now is the time to say whether Pete Alejandro Zendel has become a murderer or if he's just the mean bad boy he's been for the past decade." She edged closer until their faces were inches apart. "Did you kill the man?"

His hand lifted for a slap, but she bridged it with hers without looking away, then wagged a warning finger. "Don't you dare hit me, or I will surprise you by how well those self-defense classes have paid off. I don't think your pride can handle that in full view of your men, can it?"

He sneered at her. "I thought you were a Christian. You shouldn't hit back." A wicked smile she'd never seen turned up a corner of his lips and sent a chill over her spine.

"Yes, I am a Christian. But I won't be bullied by my own brother. You can be sure about that."

His hand swung to his side, and he stepped back as though he was also stepping away emotionally. "I'm done entertaining your tricks. I have no response to your allegations. But I do have an update about your status here."

Silence followed. When she said nothing, he continued. "I have directed the staff to know you will take over the project, henceforth known as The New Rulebook. Since our dear friend's unfortunate demise left a gap, that gap will be filled by you, and you will meet up with the deadline I provided to our clients. Since you say this is our company, its time you act like it and actively support our main project. If these terms are not agreeable to you, please feel free to quit now."

He glared at her, almost sure she would quit. Disbelief shivered through her. Tim's words were coming true. She had a choice here, and besides her, no one else would dare to oppose Pete. None.

So she leaned forward, smiled, and planted both palms on the cool table again. "Of course, I'll work on The New Rulebook. After all, I like a good challenge." She straightened, then spun toward the door, determination brimming in her. If what the scientist had shared about The New Rulebook was true, then she had double duty on her hands—build what Pete asked for, and then build in a factor to ensure its destruction—at the same time.

And she could not fail in either task. "I'll see you around." She walked out, slammed the door, and strode to the elevator, out to the parking lot and entered into her car. She prayed for God to send her a police officer she could trust without jeopardizing her safety. Then she revved her engine, slid the gear into drive, and exited the main gate.

It was time to buy that journal.

14

"So, I prophesied as I was commanded; and as I prophesied, there was a noise, and suddenly, a rattling; and the bones came together, bone to bone." –Ezekiel 37:7

~

Angel looked up from her PC when her office door creaked open. The captain leaned against the doorjamb.

"Sir?"

He scratched his short, gray beard, entered, and sunk into a chair. "Listen, I've got this man here who said he came to report Miranda Sow missing."

Her eyes widened. "Missing?"

"Yes." He nodded. "Apparently, he doesn't yet know she's dead. But, before we suspect him of complicity, I think you should listen to him. His is quite an interesting tale—it might just crack this case wide open."

She grinned widely. "Sir, I have researched everything I can, and yet, this case has frustrated me for weeks now. Where is the man now?"

He pointed behind him. "Waiting in my office."

"Do you want me to interview him there?"

The captain shook his head. "I'll escort him over. But take his statement. Matter of fact, record it and ask for his permission before doing so, please. If any of what he says is true, you're about to get swamped with leads. If so, I'll definitely be assigning more officers to support you. Good luck."

"Thank you." Angel sat up like she'd just gotten a jolt from an energy drink and searched for the recording app on her PC while she waited. She found it, then called the lab to have them back it up on their server while it recorded. When they assured her it was done, she hung up the call and waited. She preferred to secure the information in case something damaged it on her system. She tested her recorder and verified it was working. Then she announced the date and time on it after its confirmation just as both gentlemen walked in.

A tall, broad-shouldered man wearing a black UM polo shirt and rugged jeans, with a golf cap entered. His eyes were sharp, sharper than she would expect for a civilian. She stood, approached them, and smiled. "Hello, I'm Officer Angel Martinez. Please have a seat."

She pointed to a spare seat. He extended her a hand. "David Lynn. It's a pleasure to meet you." He took the seat she offered, and the captain walked out and shut the door.

She returned to her seat, glided back in, then rested her gaze on him while he tapped his foot in impatience. Finally, she cleared her throat. "My captain says you're here about a disappearance?"

He gave her a photo, and she accepted it. Yes, it was a younger image of Miranda Sow. High cheekbones, same set of blue eyes, and dark hair.

"Miranda Sow is a friend. She has not shown up at her place for the five days I've been in town, and I've checked there every day. Her office was sealed off with a Do-Not-Enter sign when I went there after checking at her house all these days. If something happened, I haven't heard anything in the news. Therefore, I came here to report her missing."

Angel eyed him. "And you say your relationship with her is...?"

He glanced away. "It's complicated."

It's complicated? Seriously? Angel was getting tired of hearing that phrase with regard to this case.

She sat back. "Listen, I'm going to ask for your permission to record this interaction. Is that all right?"

His tapping fingers went still. Then he shrugged. "Well, sure. If it will help us find her. No problem." He fidgeted and tapped his foot again. "Listen, can you please put out a statement in the media or something so someone can start looking?"

"You didn't say what your relationship with her was, Mr. Lynn. I'm going to need that to make sure you're not someone we should be looking at for a missing person."

"Call me David." His brows drew together. "Of course not. Not with the stuff she mailed me. Which was the reason I came here in the first instance."

Angel crossed her fingers. "And what did she mail you? Do you have it with you here?"

He fished in his pocket and handed her an envelope. "Here."

She accepted the letter, opened it, and extracted a single note out. Then she flipped it open and read. "I THINK THEY FOUND ME. HELP ME, DAVID." Followed by Miranda's house address scribbled at the base, along with her cell-phone number.

"Interesting." She glanced up. "Who are they? And why was she scared of them? And why were they searching for her, Mr. David?"

He shifted in his seat. "It's a long story. One I can't get into except we commence looking for her. Time is of the essence."

His impatient puff reached her ears. She had to reveal the truth to him. If Miranda trusted this man enough to inform him she was in danger, then maybe, just maybe, he might have something to say to help unravel this case.

"I'm sorry, Mr. David. But Miranda is dead."

He stared at her like she had spoken a different language, and his face turned pale.

"She was returning from a visit with a lawyer when arsonists burned down her office building, and then ran her vehicle off a valley road. She died that day. I am the officer investigating her murder, and we are trying to identify the culprits but haven't had much success. Any information you can share will help us bring Miranda some measure of justice. I'm very sorry."

He stood, wobbled a bit, then paced her office. From the manner with which he clutched his chest, it seemed like he was hyperventilating. He sat back down and stared at her with a crestfallen face. "So they did find Randy," he said slightly above a whisper.

"She's Miranda," Angel clarified for the recording to be sure they were speaking of the same person.

He nodded, then lowered his head, and a lone tear slid down his right cheek. "I know. She was Randy to me, to *us*, back then."

Angel leaned forward. "I know this has come as a shock to you and you're grieving. I also know it's a lot for you to take in, but the more we wait, the more these criminals cover their tracks. They were trying to hide something, and I want to uncover what that is. Can you help me?"

He lifted his head, wiped his cheeks, and nodded sharply. "I will. For Miranda's sake. We'll get them all."

"How many are the 'all'?" Angel held her breath.

His gaze became resolute, and again, Angel wondered if this man seated before her was a civilian, but this wasn't the time for a getting-to-know-you chat. It was time to get information, and she would not be distracted from that sworn duty.

David ran a hand through his hair, then fisted his hands, arms flexing as though about ready to exact revenge as ever. Then his gaze settled on her. "There are ten people involved. And it all began ten years ago..."

15

"*THEREFORE THE LAW IS HOLY, AND THE COMMANDMENT HOLY AND just and good.*" *–Romans 7:12*

∽

TEN YEARS EARLIER...

Miranda glanced at the science teacher sitting at the end of the bench, and her heart warmed. Their date had ended perfectly. A meal at Buena Casa de Costillas, an evening spent walking along Crescent Drive with decorative lighting, then an unexpected return to the school, where they both taught, so she could get the anxiety pills she'd forgotten to take home. Now back on school grounds, they'd left his bag and her purse in the car, locked it, and took the car keys along on the walk to the sports complex. After a ten-minute trek, she unlocked the doors with her keys, entered, and he followed her to the staff changing room where the lockers—and her pills were.

She kicked off the high heels she'd worn and set them in place next to her sweater. Then she slid her feet into the leather flats that were a constant in her staff locker.

Hardly anyone was in the sports center of Andres High School, where she was a swimming instructor. She was finishing her degree in nursing, and with one semester left, she could hardly wait to leave the part-time swimming job and start her dream career of helping people get better.

"I've had a lovely time tonight, Randy." David leaned, arms folded across his chest, against the doorjamb.

She couldn't help a chuckle. "Me too. Except when the waitress mistook us for newlyweds and served us free slices of special red-velvet cake."

He laughed and swung to face her as she searched for a bag to package her high-heeled shoes into. They were going to walk a long way back to where they parked close to the boarding school gate, and she wasn't doing it twice in one night in heels. Especially not after their nice walk in town. "Yes, it was awkward telling them they had the wrong table and that we were on our first date."

Comfortable silence stood between them.

He reached out and took her hand loosely, making her pause her action to peer in his face. "I do hope we get there, someday. If today is an indication of what me-with-you will look like, I'll give it a chance."

"I—" Miranda began saying, but a shove of the changing room doors, followed by loud rancor, and thudding feet interrupted her. She counted off the boys as they entered, and each settled their gaze on her. Ten boys, all high school students with affluent parents—donors crucial to the school's funding—seemed drunk and high on substances and perused her with unworthy intentions. The way each ran their eyes over her made it clear what they would do to her, if given the opportunity.

"Hello, Miss Randy." One boy with dark hair and blue eyes stepped out from the pack and linked a hand over her neck. "How are we doing?" When she didn't respond, he sank onto the bench and sat between where she stood and where David sat.

"How did you get in here? This space is for staff only," David queried. Her eyes met his. David, being a slender, nonathletic person, was no physical match for these boys, with muscular athletic build and who played various sports well. Moreover, he couldn't tackle all ten. She'd heard a rumor about a clique formed by these, and that they occasionally broke the rules without penalty. So, any attempt David made to defend her could earn him some violent attacks, especially since the boys were under the influence of substances.

Nevertheless, David took a step toward her. But another

boy, with light-brown hair and gray eyes, stepped between them. Then another followed him. And yet another. Until four boys were between them. They were spoiling for a fight, one she wished to prevent.

One of them, the first one who'd sat down, stood and sauntered to David. "I believe we asked the lady a question, and you were not invited to answer."

A chorus of laughter followed.

She faced them all but didn't address the boys. "Dave, I'm going to the maintenance area to find something to pack my shoes in. I'll be right back."

She stepped out the door, and one of the boys blocked the entry to prevent David from following her, which he couldn't easily do with the four bulky frames in front of him. She bit her lip. Her plan hadn't worked. They knew what she was doing—planning an escape—and the boys made sure they held onto something, *someone* she wanted, in order to ensure her return.

MIRANDA STRODE DOWN THE HALL AND TURNED RIGHT TO enter the maintenance area. She contemplated her options and didn't like any of them. First, she could call the police, if she had a phone on hand. But they would speak with the school security guards, who would inform the police that the boys had done nothing wrong.

The boys might get in minor trouble for being under the influence. However, with their parents in powerful positions, they would be freed in a little while, if they even saw a jail cell at all—and they would return for payback. Also, she wasn't going to leave David and flee.

She had one option left with the least path of conflict—wait them out—and hide here until they tired and left David. She entered a large room and spotted a coat closet. Opposite it was an open toilet. It didn't look like it was flushed so she tore out a piece of tissue paper, pushed the toilet cover over, and pressed it shut. This was the maintenance room used by the janitors who maintained the gym. Near the wall, a pile of gym laundry towels lurked in tied bags. Staff uniforms, washed and ironed, hung above the dirty laundry bags.

Good place to hide.

Miranda approached it. Never in her life did she think she would hide from some young men for potential assault. But this situation called for wisdom. Calling authorities when nothing had happened would increase the chances of something worse happening later, and she wasn't willing to risk it. She only had a semester left here. Then she was done.

She swept the uniforms aside, planted one foot behind the dirty laundry bags, and stepped beyond them to hide. Releasing the uniforms, she exhaled with a sense of relief as they swept over her upper body and hid her completely. Too bad, she'd left her purse in the car. At least, she would have had a phone to call for help. She just hadn't thought she would be in danger in a school where she worked. She thought of heading back to the parking lot, but someone who was likely a part of the boys' clique had lingered outside and might tackle her alone in the dark. So, left with no other options, she leaned against the wall, crossed her arms, and waited.

She must've fallen asleep. Because the next thing she heard was a loud bang as someone burst into the room and she jerked awake. She straightened as another set of footsteps tromped in, then another.

The stamping of feet drew closer. "Did you see her?" a young voice squeaked as more feet entered.

"Not yet, but I will. I've got plans, real plans for that chick. Did you see her legs?" the voice drawled sensually, and a low whistle followed, driving her heart into a panic.

The boys were here. They hadn't left, and their intentions were evil.

Another voice sounded closer. "When you're done, I'll take over."

Miranda clutched her chest. She'd never experienced anything like this, nor heard of it anywhere in this state. The boys moved like they were possessed by something simply intent to do evil that night.

"Then me after you. Man, it's going to be fun tonight," another boy added.

A frustrated sigh followed their fruitless search for her as buckets landed against the wall. "All that can only happen if we find her. Are you sure you saw her enter here? I won't be patient for much longer." Another object got tossed, and it knocked out the lone light bulb, throwing them into darkness. She could remember the path she had taken to reach her hiding place if she needed to run out in the dark.

More obscenities were tossed at her, and more evil plots shared. She covered her ears, disgusted by what they planned—for her. These boys were plotting a gang rape as though it was a normal occurrence.

But where was David? What had they done to him? Was someone guarding him to ensure he didn't come searching for her? He wouldn't leave her here. So, *what* happened?

That they hadn't left in what might've been thirty minutes since she left, meant they were serious. But if she had stayed there, and if they had tried anything with her and David shielded her, what would they have done to him to reach their aim?

The night was getting progressively worse. Since she had now heard their collective intentions, she would be right to call the cops, except she couldn't. And they would deny the allegation, and she would be back to square one. She might even get framed for something horrible and get locked up instead. For someone like her, struggling financially already, any legal expense was beyond her options.

Swallowing hard, she chose to stay hidden, hoping they would be unable to find her in the dark.

A very small interior room she had checked earlier, which had nothing more than a toilet and washing sink in it, creaked open. Then someone slammed it shut. She listened as each boy dug deep into items, opened places, tossed objects, searching for her. She'd once heard about avoiding dark places because something bad could happen. Tonight, that couldn't be truer. She wrapped her arms around herself with desperate fingers and held her breath any time someone drew close.

Their search grew more frantic, impatience raising their voices. She wished she could flee but felt safest staying put as her heart pounded in her chest.

Then a hand pressed against her face, and she was sure her heart almost stopped beating. "How do you find something warm-blooded and alive on a cold, dark night, boys?" a boy mocked. "You wet your hands with cold water and trail the heat signal. I found her."

Her heart sank further. His hand clamped like a cold vice plastered against her face, and even though a uniform separated them, his clench on her face was strong, pressing deep into her eyes.

It was time to run. Or die.

Miranda slammed a hand against the wall, jumped over where she knew the dirty laundry was near her feet, then pushed his hand away. She ran toward the door and reached it only to come into the view of flooding light from the outer hallway. Two boys, who lay on the floor near the door—

drunk and almost passed out—glanced up, and their eyes met hers.

"Hey!" one of them shouted.

But she didn't wait. She jumped high into the air and narrowly missed their hands lifted to clamp her feet to make her tumble. Her feet landed in the hallway. She ran toward the changing room where she'd left David as a trail of shouts followed. Curses rained behind her, and the other boys gave chase.

"David! They want to gang rape me!" She saw David appear at the doorway, punch the boy who stood in his way, dive out, and run toward her.

Caught between the boys chasing her, and the one racing toward David as he neared her, Miranda knew one thing— with her revelation, the chances of them leaving this night alive were slim—and if they did, she would be on the run for the rest of her life.

It was going to be a night that would change her life forever.

16

"Do not be overcome by evil, but overcome evil with good."
–*Romans 12:21*

It wasn't until David stopped speaking that Angel realized she had stopped breathing. She drew in breath sharply and planted a hand on her chest as she slowly exhaled. "Wow." She settled against her chair. "So, this was what Miranda said to you, I'm guessing?"

He nodded. "Yes, almost word for word."

"So," Angel leaned up, "how did you both escape?"

He paused for a moment, then glanced at her with that intent look. "We didn't. Two security guards, who were making their rounds, got there just then and radioed the situation in. They asked us what the problem was. While Randy cried, I informed them, that they had planned to gang rape her. The guards called the police, and when they arrived, the boys said they were simply talking to each other and not about Randy. So, her case was dismissed."

"I'm assuming the story didn't end there as Miranda is now dead."

"Not nearly. They fired Randy two weeks later. Then I helped her land a job at another school. But she started receiving death threats, and someone broke into her house. So I asked some guys, and they helped us get her a new ID, with a new driver's license, and she fled. We chose to separate to save her life and to stop the boys whose parents had come to query Randy before she was let go at the other job. Clearly, she was a loose end they wanted to take care of to protect the boys' futures."

"At the expense of Miranda's." Angel brushed her hair back.

"Exactly. Randy chose to stay in the state to take care of her elderly grandma but changed everything else. And moved to an area where she least expected anyone to come looking. We did everything possible to make it hard enough for anyone to find her, and we hoped the last place they'd expect her to be would be within the same state. We also had little time to help her disappear so it was rushed and mistakes were possible."

"Well, if it helped to conceal her for ten years, then you both did a pretty good job. What prompted them to come looking for her?"

"I'm not sure. That's what I hoped to find out."

Angel opened a drawer to get a notepad and grabbed a pen. "Can you write down the names of the ten boys if you know them, please?"

"Sure." He nodded and accepted the items. "I could never forget their names. They endangered a lady I loved and denied me a chance to spend my life with her."

Her heart hurt for the love those two sacrificed to protect Miranda. And as he wrote, Angel prayed that, if any of the boys were involved in the death of Miranda Sow, she would nab them in time.

ANGEL DROVE HOME LOOKING FORWARD TO ONE THING— hitting the pillow. It was late. Following her interview with David, she was happy to make some headway on the murder and arson investigation. She had two possible directions to focus on—Miranda's client files and David's list of ten boys, who were now men.

Because the first attempt against Miranda had been to burn down the office before killing her, Angel suspected the culprit was hidden somewhere within Miranda's clientele.

After going through the files with the clients' names and

hoping for a miracle, she came to the same conclusion as Mr. Spencer. There were some powerful people in her client list, including past governors, state legislators, and famous actors. After obtaining the right clearances, she was allowed access to some sealed files tonight.

That took things to a whole other level. She unlocked a list of eight people who might possibly want Miranda dead. Those eight sealed-file client names listed two drug dealers; a gang kingpin who was already in prison but, after his recent release, had paid her a visit; a doctor who was sued for medical malpractice; two teachers, one who manipulated scores for students in exchange for favors, another who threatened a student with a deadly weapon; and three officers on administrative leave for excessive use of force in conducting various arrests.

Then the last one shocked her.

Tommy Moore—a promising candidate for the US House of Representatives, who was new to politics. The elections were happening soon, and he could be a prime suspect if he had something to hide. She'd dig into his files in detail tomorrow since the lawyer had said Miranda mentioned a congressional candidate. First, she would check her notes for the exact name tomorrow.

Stifling a yawn, she pulled into her driveway and parked outside her garage, meaning to drive inside after she'd gathered her purse, files, and other items. She leaned over to retrieve her purse from the front seat, when an object smashed into her right passenger window and rained shattered glass onto the seat.

Angel ducked beneath the steering wheel. She inched her head up slowly and found shards of glass all around her —and someone running toward the back of her house. So, she grabbed her phone, jumped out, then gave chase.

She reached her backyard, leading to her neighbor's backyard, too, where a rustle of leaves jostled in the distance. She chased along, but after jumping the low fencing and watching the figure disappear into a small path, she found it tough to breathe and had to stop to catch her breath. Obviously, her body hadn't healed enough to sustain a prolonged foot chase. She was also alone and chasing a criminal on foot, and in the dark, which wasn't too safe.

So, she relented much against her wish, but choosing to avoid an earful from Pierce, she doubled back to her car, then called the station. While waiting for a squad car, she gathered her things and walked around her car to see what she'd been attacked with. A piece of rock had been thrown at her window. She sighed but avoided the urge to touch it without gloves.

Soon, other officers arrived and cordoned off the area, studying the damage to her vehicle. An hour later, they had searched the surrounding areas but didn't find the suspect. Knowing he or she was likely long gone, she thanked them for coming and for stationing an officer to watch her place in case the suspect showed up again.

Her front door opened, and John emerged with puffy eyes. Had he been asleep this whole time? The way he rubbed his eyes suggested so. Considering he typically left for work quite early most times, she wouldn't be surprised that he'd been sleeping and hadn't heard a thing. He walked toward her, now wide-eyed. "What's going on?"

She sighed as the last officer waved goodbye before getting into the squad car. "Someone threw a piece of rock at my window, crushing the glass."

His brow furrowed. "What? You should've called me."

She shrugged. "You're not a cop. That would've put you in danger. Anyway, I chased him but he got away. So I called the station to report the attack."

"I'm glad you're okay." He waved her forward. "Let's get out of this cold."

As they entered the house and locked the door, Angel rubbed shivers from her arms, relieved to be safe. She crossed to the dining table, settled her weapon's belt, car keys, and purse on it.

An inviting aroma wafted into her nostrils from the kitchen area. "Well, don't we have a surprise chef in the house? What did you cook or order?"

"Not ordered, I cooked." He grinned, and some pride curved his smile deeper into his cheeks since she'd smelled and appreciated the aroma. "Since you did all the cooking while we were growing up, I thought I would make you a meal for a change. It's your birthday, sis."

Angel face-palmed herself. "I forgot my own birthday. Great."

"We remembered for you." John loosely clutched her arm and led her toward the kitchen where five tall cards stood at the kitchen table, with a cake at the center of it. "Everyone wants you to know how much we appreciate all of your sacrifice. So, these are handwritten cards from each of us, saying thank you for your sacrifices over these years. We love and appreciate you. You are the best big sister in the whole world."

Angel teared up and wrapped her arms around him. His words and action hugged her heart even tighter. "Awww, John. You're going to make me cry. This means a lot to me. I can't believe you guys pulled this off. Thank you for at least remembering, because I definitely forgot."

"Poor Angel. Always saving everyone else." He teased and she laughed. "Well, now we all join to save you." A serious look smoothed his face. "Seriously, I love you, sis. You mean a lot to me, and I know the extent of your sacrifice."

He swallowed, and his head dipped a bit. "I know that, had you not been busy taking care of us, you would've been married by now. I'm sorry for the delay you encountered, and I pray God will lead the right man into your life at His right time. We're praying for you."

She hugged him again, this time, unable to keep the

happy tears from wetting her cheeks. "Thank you, Johnny. And I love you too. I will call the others tomorrow." Her other siblings must've gone to sleep, and she didn't wish to wake them up.

He propelled her forward. "Okay, come and cut your cake. I've been resisting diving into this delicious temptation while waiting up all day. Well, all night, too, since I got home from work a few hours ago. I must've fallen asleep on the couch."

That's what she thought.

John settled a knife next to the cake and set two flat plates on the counter. Angel rounded the table, picked up the knife, and sliced down the middle. "Thank You, Lord Jesus, for the grace to see another year. I give all the glory to You. May the coming years glorify You in my life. I'm very grateful for all You have done, and also for those You have not done. They all work together for my good. Thank You, Lord, in Jesus' mighty name, amen."

A slight hesitation trailed her prayer, which surprised her because these days John said amen to her prayers. Then, as she glanced up, John smiled. "Amen, sis."

She cut a slice for her and for him as he brought out the ravioli pasta from the fridge, along with spaghetti meatballs, and heated those in the microwave. The aroma alone had her mouth watering. John took his plate with cake, grabbed plastic forks for them, then sat down across from her.

The sweetness of the chocolate cake melted in her

mouth, and her shoulders loosened. When had been the last time she'd relaxed like this? Her last birthday? Maybe not that long, but it sure felt like a long time.

John tapped the fork on his plate. "I have a question about the prayer you just prayed."

"Sure. Ask me." John had been ravenously studying Scripture since his conversion to Christ. If she couldn't answer a question, she directed it to her pastor. "What about it?"

"You'd thanked God for the things He had done."

She nodded. "Yes."

"But you also thanked Him for the things He didn't do. Why? Are you supposed to thank God when bad things happen too?"

She chuckled, wiped her mouth, and took a sip of water from a glass he set next to her plate just as the microwave chimed and he stood to retrieve the food. She waited for him to return with it. "You know what, John? Yes, we should. Scripture tells us to give Him thanks in *every* situation, not just the ones we like. Why? Because all things—the good, the bad, the ugly, including the unforgivable—work together, not alone, but *together* for our good. If we believe this, then we can and should thank God in every situation."

"Interesting," John replied between chews.

"Yes. It is." She poised her fork in the air while resisting the temptation to indulge in more cake. "I'll tell you three major things I've learned in my life. One, no matter how a circumstance looks, Jesus has the final Word. Two, Jesus is Lord above every situation, no matter how bad it seems. Third, God is good, and no depth of evil occurrences can change that. I grasp these as my weapons of overcoming the evil I see every day in my job, and I know that, no matter how things look here, these three things hold true."

She counted off on her fingers for emphasis. "One, Jesus has the final Word. Two, Jesus is Lord above every situation. Three, God is good."

John's fork had frozen midair while she talked, like he was absorbing her words. "Jesus has the final Word. Jesus is Lord above every situation. God is good."

"Exactly."

"Thank you." He pointed at her dish of pasta. "Now, please eat your food before this turns from dinner into breakfast."

Angel laughed and tossed a fallen piece of cake at his face.

He eyed her narrowly. "Oh, no, you didn't." He finger-scooped some icing and flung it at her, and it got her ear after she ducked.

She set her fork down and staggered her stance. This was shaping up to be a food-fight kind of birthday. And after the long, bitter weeks she'd had, a food fight would be sweet. Angel eagerly dipped her fingers into the cake, scooped up more icing, and returned the favor.

17

"HE DELIVERS THE POOR IN THEIR AFFLICTION, AND OPENS THEIR *ears in oppression." –Job 36:15*

~

THE FOLLOWING DAY, ANGEL STRODE TOWARD HER NEW POLICE cruiser, struggling to contain her anger. She had just left the congressional candidate's campaign office and almost had a cease-and-desist letter slammed in her face for querying the man over the phone. He was out of state for campaign matters, but his staffers were able defenders of him. Their candidate was perfect, they said, and had done no wrong nor harmed Miranda Sow.

She'd called her captain to intervene, and after he called

the higher powers, two hours later, the candidate returned and she was able to sit down with him. He'd basically denied ever having had a shrink or needing one—his words, not hers.

Which meant, she needed to find out why he'd gone to a psychiatrist. Then she'd practically gotten shoved out the door.

She entered her car, slammed the door, and returned to the SSPD. She got right into the files they had retrieved, pulled out his case file, and read through it. Then she flipped to the back of the file and froze before drawing the folder closer and tipping it to the setting sunlight streaming through the passenger window. Was that...? Yes, a scratched-out note with a date of...wait...a few days before Miranda's death?

She took the lone sheet to the captain. "Look, I think we found something. I'm going to need some help figuring out what was written and then scratched out."

"Get the folks in the lab on it right away." He nodded. "This man keeps resisting us at every turn. We'll get to the bottom of this. Great job."

With a nod, she proceeded to the lab, handed over the sheet, then went to grab some lunch with Tim. She'd been surprised when he had asked her out to lunch. But having no other engagements, she accepted.

When she arrived at Olive Garden, she easily spotted his dark hair peeking above the seat close to the door. She walked past the hanging plant suspended above the hostess desk, passed a couple being served their meals, and turned a slight corner toward Tim. Then she caught the whiff of spicy Calabrian chicken breadsticks sandwich, and her mouth watered.

Once he saw her, he smiled and pulled out a seat. "Hi, Angel. Please have a seat."

"Thanks for choosing a place so close to the station." She sank into the chair he had pulled out, rubbing her neck as a waiter approached. Hopefully, their food would be served soon, and they'd have enough time for a quick chat. "It's good to see you, Tim."

"You seem like you've worked hard enough for one day already. Those bags under your pretty eyes say a lot."

Chuckling, she blinked in surprise that he had noticed her eyes and called them pretty. "You can say that again. A murder investigation is never easy. People close up when police officers show up, and all you're after is the truth. I want this case sorted, and I'm determined to see it to the end."

"And there's our Angel. Always chasing the truth. John told me someone had attacked your car last night, so it's good to see you're fine. I've been praying for you."

"Thank you. I can use all the prayers I can get."

"Say, how is John doing? He's been busy, I presume, and honestly, so have I. As a result, we haven't spoken for a bit."

She smiled as the waiter took their orders, then left. "John is doing good, great actually. It's such a remarkable difference between who he was and who he now is in Christ.

He's so responsible now it's hard to compare him to his past. I'm grateful, too, for the role you played in his conversion. Who knew all of that can come out of a job recommendation, huh?"

"Life is full of godly surprises." Tim played loosely with the edge of his napkin. "How about we add one more surprise to that?"

A waiter served their trademark free bread and set a bowl of salad at the center of their table. She wondered what Tim had in mind but refused to guess. She sucked in her lower lip. "How do you mean, Tim?"

He cleared his throat. "This morning, after speaking with John, I realized that time waits for nobody. The risk you faced with the attack weeks ago and the one last night showed me I couldn't wait any longer before saying this."

"Saying what?" She picked up the serving fork and served herself some salad. She took her fork and played with the food for want of something to center her. The longer Tim waited to speak, the more she wondered what could be so hard.

Finally, he cleared his throat and set a gentle hand on hers, and it stilled. "I want to ask you out on a date, Angel." Her gaze trailed his words to his eyes and held. "If you're not in a relationship." Hope glistened in his gaze.

Her eyes widened as he withdrew his hand and settled it on his lap, then gave her a disarming smile. "Tim, are you serious? I mean, I want to be sure this isn't a spur-of-the-moment thing."

He nodded, and the bounce of those Italian curls added certainty to his words. "Yes, I'm sure. It took me a while to pray through to know this is what God wanted. I want to go on a date with you, Angel. Would you give me the honor?"

She thought for a moment and chuckled. "If you're sure Jesus led you to ask, then, I'd say yes."

A vigorous nod followed. "I am certain."

"All right then." Surprised this had become more than a lunch between friends but had turned into something better, Angel wished she didn't have to go back to the station because all she wanted to do now was jump and squeal for joy. But she simply shrugged and maintained her composure.

Soon, their food arrived. But the coming date lingered pleasantly at the back of her mind as she ate.

She silently thanked God for it and prayed that, whenever it happened, it would be according to His will and for both their good. Caught by this surprise, she gladly enjoyed a happy surprise for a change.

VIOLET ARRIVED HOME FROM WORK AND KNEW SHE'D HAD IT. Pete had cut off her access to the Executive Floor, made her have to sign in each time she entered and exited the lab, and basically reduced her status to a regular employee.

Confronting him yet again had yielded no positive outcome, leaving her with a broken spirit and a determined mind. Yet she had cooperated and worked very hard on The New Rulebook project. He had a goal, and she had hers—and both were polar opposites. It was almost finished. But he'd asked her twice if she was hiding anything, and she equally asked *him* if *he* was hiding anything. Of course, he hadn't admitted to having a hand in the death of their deceased employee, but he was never going to tell her the truth, so that became her sole leverage.

Today was the final straw for her. And while she had earlier contemplated allowing the program to run on a limited basis, the required separate adjustments would flag her actions to Pete.

That was why, today, she completed her construction of what would ensure its destruction. And she didn't regret it. She just hadn't safely extracted it out of Cortexe Corp. yet. Running against her brother's project pained her, but he'd left her to choose between his ambitions and the public good. It was clear that involving authorities would set alarms off and the deeply interested parties wouldn't quit until the program was re-created. Her only option now, knowing she was the one person who currently understood the program fully—was to ensure its destruction. But accomplishing it in a way that didn't alert Pete was as tough as climbing Mount Everest unguided. He had eyes—and guards—everywhere and tracked her movements within the complex.

Violet set her purse near her couch, kicked off her black pumps, and relaxed into the cushions. She then bowed her head and poured her heart out to God. She'd used her lunchtime to visit their family lawyer yesterday, asking about the possibility of challenging Pete legally.

But their lawyer had indicated that any move she made to challenge Pete would be public and could attract severe backlash against them both. He'd advised that they sort out their differences privately, which wouldn't happen in the near future.

She sighed, stayed near the couch, and literally prayed all evening. She was tired. Of Pete. Of his harassment. Of being in the right, but overshadowed by her brother. Of having to choose between getting him to do what was right or having their family made into a public spectacle.

She needed divine guidance. So, she turned to the Word. For another hour, she just read the word of God and sought His leading for her decisions. Exhausted, she sipped some water, set it down, then continued praying. At some point, she slid down to the floor and rested her back against the couch.

She pulled her hair into a bond with a rubber band, and when her fingers caught at the tip of it, she tugged at it until it came through. Then she huffed and massaged her neck. Why was she struggling to maintain long hair? She'd better head to the salon and get a haircut tomorrow. Decided, she rose, made some dinner, ate, and then went to bed.

In the next week or so, with God's grace and guidance, she would finalize her work on the project and be free of it. For good. Then she could move on with her life.

Angel dipped her chin and studied the list of names in her hand. She'd met with David two more times to inquire about Miranda, and based on her own investigations, all the facts he presented played true. The ten boys had stuck together after leaving high school. They had even bought homes close to each other and led secretive lives. No online social media accounts, or such, which, for a bunch of thirty-or-so-year-olds, was odd.

Visiting all ten this week had revealed a mellowed-down nature for all but one of them, who got prickly when she mentioned Randy. She noted his reaction and jotted it down. They all denied having done anything to hurt Randy. Two claimed not to remember who she was, but their body language betrayed the lies.

She sat at her desk and toyed with her pen—*was* there a missing link? The only persons on both the client lists and the boys' list that she hadn't contacted personally were the two famous actors. It would be challenging, but before throwing up her hands in the air, she was going to shake those giant trees and see if any leaves fell down.

18

"DO NOT FEAR THEREFORE; YOU ARE OF MORE VALUE THAN MANY *sparrows.*" –*Matthew 10:31*

∾

THE PAST WEEK HAD BEEN THE MOST HECTIC VIOLET EVER worked, but that wasn't her present challenge.

It was this man.

Violet sat across from the tall man in plain clothes, sipping tea on the Silver Stone Metropolitan Transit train across from her as it chugged down the tracks and wondered what to make of him. The scenic view of green grasslands she typically enjoyed whenever she commuted by train to clear her mind from the pressures of her job was far from her vision as she tried to assess the fellow while he behaved as though all was well and he'd done nothing wrong. In addition, she'd asked a driver to send her car home for her while she commuted to protect this fellow, but she still wasn't sure what to make of him.

He set his cup down and, as though sensing her perusal, raised his head and locked his eyes in with hers. They had a certain kindness, but she was bent on finding out his plans for her company.

He smiled as if to ease her worries, and the dimple on his smooth cheek raised her heart rate, though she didn't return the smile. First, they just met hours earlier, and she literally saved his life from Pete. Secondly, he had to explain what he was doing sneaking into Cortexe Corp. and pretending to be an intern. Yes, she had prayed for God to send her a good cop, someone she could trust, but this wasn't the way she'd expected Him to do it.

She curled her arms and sat back, watching his every move and trying not to be distracted. His muscles bulged every time he moved his arms, definitely distracting her from her goal. What was happening to her? This was definitely not what she wanted, especially not today. She cleared her throat loudly. "You said you're a cop. What were you doing snooping around on my company grounds without a search warrant and pretending to be an intern?"

He settled a hairy arm on the small table between them and smiled warmly again. The warmth in his eyes was doing things to her belly that she didn't want to admit.

Now was not the time for romantic admiration. She was at war with her brother who theoretically was working to destroy the world—with a click—as she strove to save it. "I want to thank you for saving my life back there. I'm grateful."

His voice moved like silk over her heart, and she found herself nodding in acceptance with little hesitation—and with a small smile. "Sure. You're welcome. My brother wouldn't be that magnanimous had you been taken to him instead. So, I'm asking you yet again, what you were seeking to find? I bought this ride home just for this time with you, so I hope you won't waste my time." She had to make it home on time to mail Tim an old letter. He *was* frankly the only person she trusted now, but she hadn't heard from him in almost one week. Moreover, the letter in question was from her dad's drawer. Seemingly old, it was written in Spanish, and some of the terms used in it sounded contradictory. Confused, she wanted Tim to take a look at it now—rather than wait until his return. Her gaze returned to the man across from her.

"I–I was searching for any information about something called, The Rulebook," he flatly said.

Oh, he meant what's now called The New Rulebook. But how did he know about it? Her ears perked.

He lifted both hands in the air. "Listen, I know how weird this sounds, but I've got a dead body in the morgue with those words written on him. A former employee of Cortexe

Corp.—by the way. I think those two things are connected to why he died. My captain wants to see what you or anyone here knows about it. Your website is pretty bare, and there was no other way to gain access. So I entered as an intern. My apologies. And if you know nothing, then I'm sorry to have wasted your time." His gaze lingered on her face as though both studying it and admiring it. Then he sat back, and an announcement rasped overhead, saying her stop was coming up.

But if this man was a cop, and she needed a cop to talk to, maybe he was the right person.... She could at least tease the edges of trust with a few facts, see how things shape up, and then know whether she could trust him fully. Or not. "My stop is next. There is a Mexican restaurant I usually grab dinner at." She thought of the men she was sure Pete could have hired to trail her every move and knew she had to be careful. Then she added, "If you follow me there, we can talk."

"Yes, I'll go with you. The station will send someone to drop off an unmarked police cruiser, with the keys inside for me there. I can use that to drop you off later." His shoulders dropped in relief. "And thank you."

She bit her lip at her next brazen suggestion. "But we need to be careful in case my brother is watching." She saw a cross and John 3:16 tattooed along his elbow. Then her gaze returned to his face. "You'll act like we're on a date, and I'm sure we'll be fine."

She watched his reaction as a smile broke out wider than before. "A date? With a beautiful lady like you? That shouldn't be a problem at all."

Surely, her cheeks were burning with the way he swept her another admiring glance. Then a serious look overcast his gaze. "Then we can talk about why you need to hide from your brother. No one should be made to feel unsafe, especially not from one of their own. No one."

This time, the smile reached her heart. "Of course, you'll say that. You're a cop."

They exited as soon as the train stopped, looped their hands as they walked, arrived at the restaurant within minutes, and entered through the curved archway. Violet liked the floor here, painted to look like beautiful cascading stacked decks, while the hanging colorful red, green, and white lights over each table added to its ambiance. The atmosphere was usually calm and with no loud music, perfect for her to sit and clear her head whenever she had to.

She waved to Amanda, one of her favorite waitresses, and the woman waved back from behind the counter as she claimed her seat opposite the cop. While they ordered, she contemplated how much information to reveal while still protecting Pete. Maybe just enough to test him....

"Ma'am, can I take your order please?" a waiter holding a pen and a notepad asked, interrupting her thoughts.

"Yes. I would like a—" A hand tapped her shoulder, and

she turned to see a scraggy-looking figure. Then recognition hit, and her eyes rounded as she lurched to her feet. "Tim?"

She hugged his thin frame, a far cry from the healthy man who'd left the US months earlier. "Good to see you. I've missed you, bro." She had missed him. But she was struggling not to reveal her shock at his change. He hadn't said a word yet so she beckoned him to sit. "Please join us."

He seemed to think about it, glance behind him toward the entrance. Then he swallowed hard. "I can't stay, Vi. I need to warn you first. I didn't want to lead them to your house so I came here, hoping to find you. How I prayed you would come!"

Struggling not to cover her mouth over how emaciated he was, she placed a hand on her chest. "Tim, what are you talking about? Who are they?"

He cast his eyes back like he expected someone to show up. "It's a long story, but the short version is this—there is a link between the contract I'm researching under in Mexico and your dad."

"My dad?" She pressed a hand to her chest. "He never lived in Mexico."

"Sorry, not really him, but his poem. I remember you saying he'd never lived in Mexico. But something definitely ticked someone off when I followed my results from your tests. I mentioned his poem in my class and asked them to translate it into Spanish. One month later, things began to happen."

"Things? Like what *things*?" She fought the urge to turn away from his stale breath as a waiter passed and gave Tim a questioning look. Tim was her friend and she would stand by him no matter what.

He planted a hand on his hip. "Random items began missing from my office. At first, I thought it was a thief. Then threatening calls followed, asking about the source of the poem, but...in Spanish."

"Wow." Violet touched his elbow near her.

"I'm not sure what this is about, but it seems I might've ruffled some powerful feathers because someone who's well connected is now after me." He paused and let his arm drop, as did hers from his elbow. "I never told anyone it was your poem or your dad's. So, they think it's mine, and they're pursuing me."

"Because of a poem?" the cop spoke for the first time.

Violet cast him an impatient glance—she hadn't introduced them yet! "Sorry, my mistake. Tim, meet Detective Mike Argan of the Silver Stone Police Department. He's investigating The New Rulebook. Mike, meet Tim Santiago. He's a seasoned archeologist with a specialization on South America. He's also my prayer partner and friend."

With the introductions done, she turned to Tim and patted on the chair. "Tim, I know you might be scared, and you're not making much sense right now. Plus, I think you could use a meal and a shower. But why don't you sit down first, and we can..."

He shook his head vigorously, and his dark curls bounced. He settled a hand on Violet's shoulder. "Vi, are you listening to me? Someone is trying to kill me because they think I'm you. If they knew you are the real owner of that poem, guess what will happen?"

"Did you talk to the police?" Mike folded his arms across his chest.

"In Mexico, yes. By the time I arrived at home, DEA was waiting, saying someone called in that a drug deal was going down in my house, which wasn't true. I didn't suspect foul play until I entered the house that night, and all the communication wires had been cut, phones disconnected, and a warning spray painted on my kitchen wall. 'WHAT IS THE POEM? WHO ARE YOU? DON'T CALL THE COPS OR WE WILL ANSWER.'"

Tim sighed and his shoulders hunched. "So, I fled. Not knowing who to trust, I didn't call the cops. I also didn't want to call you and get you into trouble. Instead of flying, I hitch-hiked for a whole week to reach here."

Violet blinked. "From Mexico?"

"Yes, virtually, after I spent the cash I had. All the way from Mexico. I left everything behind—phones, luggage, *everything*. I couldn't risk withdrawing money from the ATM. When I arrived at Silver Stone today, I slept at a metro station not far from here for a few hours instead of going home in case someone knew my US address. Then I remembered you usually come by this restaurant, and I chose to risk showing up and warn you."

Violet felt her brow draw together. "But my dad never told me the origin of the poem."

"Ask him," Mike said.

"He's dead."

"Oops. Sorry about that. How do we handle this then?" Mike turned to Tim. "I can take you down to the station and place you in protective custody. Will you prefer that?"

Tim appeared to think for a second as his brows arched upward. Then he nodded. "Yes. That is fine. But if we can pass by my place first, I'll appreciate it. At least, I can get some money from the house and a change of clothes."

"No problem." They rose, and Mike tipped the waiter for their free drinks since they had eaten nothing, and they rode in his police cruiser and, about a half hour later, drove into Realms Street where Tim lived.

She spun to speak. But he had dozed off, and his head leaned slightly against her shoulder. Her heart ached for her friend suffering through no fault of his own. It crushed her heart that, because of a family relic—*her* family relic—his life was turned upside down. But as they rounded a few turns and approached his house, she tapped his arm lightly. "Tim, wake up. We're here."

He lifted his head, popped his eyelids open, and wiped his face with a hand, then sat up straight.

Mike was easing in to park across the house, maybe to

survey the area first, when she thought she heard a hissing sound. Across the way, a black Chevrolet approached slowly, then zoomed past them, driving much faster than it should in an inner street. Mike flicked on his police siren. They revved up their speed in response, and he called it in through the radio.

Then, behind them, an explosion rocked the road.

19

❧

VIOLET CLUTCHED HER SEAT BELT AS MIKE HIT THE BRAKES,
the tires screeched, and she turned to see what it was. She
closed a hand over her mouth. Tim's car—parked in the
street-side curb—erupted in flames. Tim had taken out the
car's battery, so it wasn't an electrical fault. Someone set his
car ablaze on purpose, and that had her heart pounding.

Her eyes rounding, she gripped the front seat's headrest.

"Okay, this is definitely not a coincidence. Something is
going on here." Mike grabbed the radio, updated the SSPD,
and asked for a firefighters' truck to be sent. Then he turned.

"I want to know everything about The New Rulebook, Violet."

She wasn't waiting. "I'll tell you everything." If danger was around the corner—against her or Tim or both—she'd do everything to stave it off.

"And about the poem," Mike added. "And about your late dad, who appears to be at the center of this."

"Yes, everything actually began in Mexico, two years ago, while I was on vacation with Tim and Pete."

"Okay, thank you. I'd like to hear more." He spun to Tim. "I don't know what you unearthed in Mexico. But tell me everything that happened since you arrived there and began digging into Violet's family's poem. And maybe we can get ahead of these manipulators."

He glanced at both of them. "Seems we've got a poem they think is worth killing for—why? Meanwhile, I'm taking you both to the station for Tim's account of his targeting and," he turned to Violet, "for us to wrap up our first date."

"Uh...." She opened her mouth to respond, but only managed a soft "oooh."

"I'm teasing." He tapped a finger on the armrest. "But not about getting to the bottom of these issues."

"Oh good." Her shoulders dropped as she exhaled. "And Tim and I will cooperate with you fully."

"After all, our lives depend on it," Tim whispered, clearly shaken. He curled an arm around his midsection and shivered, then gulped. His slim frame curved slightly, possibly under the pressure of the entire ordeal he had already been through.

She reached out an arm and touched his hand, smiling a little. "It's going to be all right, by God's grace, Tim. I believe it."

He gave a bare nod as her hand dropped. "I had locked up a few things in the car in case anyone broke into the house while I was away. There were carved Ethiopian wooden art pieces in the trunk. I guess they will be burned too. To me, those are—irreplaceable. Including the gift you brought me from London."

"The miniature female diver sculpture? I know you like it and carry it everywhere. We can always get another one next time we pass through London." But that was poor comfort as his form curved even further and lines deepened on his face. She squeezed his shoulder. "I'm so sorry for your losses. I would take care of this if I could. I can't believe I got you into all this. It's my fault."

He shook his head. "Don't you dare say that. You didn't burn my car—they did. And whoever 'they' are, we will find them and make them pay."

Mike veered into traffic, just as the same black Chevy showed back up again.

And a bullet pierced her window and lodged in the front seat's armrest, missing her by a hair's breath.

"Shots fired!" Violet shouted and ducked her head.

But she was barely done speaking before more shots followed. Mike raced forward, but the shots pelting the cruiser shattered the side mirror and back window. The glass rained onto the street like popcorn. But that slowed the Chevy further as it veered sideways to avoid it, gaining Mike some distance.

Soon, Mike expertly maneuvered them several feet ahead of the black Chevy. Then he swerved to a side street, and melted into traffic, then navigated into yet another, even while he radioed for backup.

She exhaled in relief, although her heart still thudded. Then something damp wet her thigh. She trailed the source upward, and it rested on the blood flowing from Tim's shoulder onto her thigh. "Tim!" She lifted his shoulder with a hand, her breath clogging her throat. He'd gotten hit. Blood stained his blue shirt and arm. Pressing her palm to the epicenter, Violet stifled a gasp as blood seeped through her fingers. "Tim is bleeding. Please call for an ambulance."

Mike rushed a hand to his radio and did so.

Violet clutched Tim's shirt and prayed harder than she ever had, that her friend would not die. She prayed furiously, then pressed her lime-green scarf on it to stem the bleeding, but when Tim's blood soaked the scarf in a few minutes she cried out for help. "We can't lose Tim! Let them hurry please." She propped up Tim's chin as his head started drooping and he mumbled confusing words in slurred speech. "Stay with me, Tim. Please don't die."

"An ambulance is on the way." Mike veered off that street into an open commercial parking garage. Then flashing his badge and identifying himself, he ordered the security personnel to close the entrance. They scrambled to obey.

He turned off the vehicle and stepped down. Mike rounded the cruiser and helped her set Tim—who was now unconscious—on the ground gently. Then he lifted his gaze to hers, worry lines creasing his forehead as he darted his gaze between hers and the entrance. "As it stands right now, I'm outgunned until backup arrives, and I don't wish for anything else to go wrong here. I want Tim to live, but we can't make a sound until more police officers arrive with the ambulance. I can't risk losing you, too, without knowing what I'm up against. So, please, start talking."

Violet nodded and knelt on the opposite side, still pressing a hand on Tim's wound, while Mike stemmed the bleeding on Tim's chest, both working as a team. "I understand, and I'll tell you all I remember."

So she began. "Pete, Tim, and I were on vacation a while ago in Mexico..."

20

"Death and life are in the power of the tongue. And those who love it will eat its fruit." –Proverbs 18:21

One week after interviewing both popular actors David had mentioned, and visiting the high school in question, then leaving with more questions than answers, Angel decided all trails led to these grounds—the Fortitude Homes Estate. Observing the affluence surrounding her in the sprawling Odenton, Maryland estate, home of actress Liberty Stone, Angel managed not to allow her mouth to drop open. Angel had expected a small house since this wasn't the actress's permanent home. But if there was anything people knew about Liberty, only her love of guns and shooting, apparently, surpassed her name and affluence.

A Lamborghini sat parked under a zinc-roofed detachment, beneath a tree, in the expansive gun range, which doubled as her home here. Standing about a hundred feet from the parking area beyond the gate where Angel left her partner sitting in the police cruiser—ready to proceed inside should anything go wrong—she spotted four buildings within the estate. An immaculate, white, four-story mansion, the shooting range, front and center, and a real garage—not the small canopy under the tree—three times the size of a middle-class home.

Arriving early in the morning meant the roads had been clear and the drive less than fifty minutes rather than two hours. She hoped Liberty would cooperate, since Angel had avoided a public display of force, as requested. They had come in plain clothes and drove an unmarked cruiser to avoid rousing media interest from those folks camped outside the estate.

Angel pulled out her radio, tuned the right dial, and spoke to her partner. "Pierce, I'm outside her shooting range. She suggested we meet in front of it, though I'm not sure why."

Static came over the radio. "Copy that. I'm here, armed and ready should you require backup. I'm keeping the SSPD looped, just in case." The line fell silent before his voice came over, softer this time. "Be careful, Angel."

Of course, he was caring and would say so. "I will. If you need to enter, here's the gate entry code." She dictated it to him. "And the shooting range is out front by your right. You can't miss it. Just walk toward where you see targets set up close to the distant boundary bushes."

"Okay. If you can't radio, keep me posted via text messaging."

"Will do. Over and Out." Angel visually tracked indented steps in the sandy path ahead to a structure on the far left. With its flat roof and large windows facing the target props, it had to be the shooting range. In contrast to the rolling lawns of the estate grounds—manicured to perfection—gravel and sand lined the shooting range and the path leading up to it.

But where was Liberty? Facing the shooting range, Angel contemplated approaching the main building.

She spun a moment later when the low whir of a vehicle purred closer. Behind her, a golf cart pulled to a stop, and Liberty alighted. Instantly recognizable from her celebrity photos, the lady came close, offered a dazzling smile, and extended a sleek hand. Angel now understood why she got all the attention she did. "Hi, Officer Martinez, welcome to my humble home."

Tall and hourglass shaped, with bronze skin and long dark hair curling to her waist, she was part Jewish, but few people knew that. Instead, her Italian heritage was publicized since her family had fled Eastern Europe in the 1930s, migrated to Italy, and lived there until they moved to the US.

Angel almost spat at the description of the estate as a "humble home". Her own house could fit that description better, not this. Nevertheless, she accepted the handshake and smiled too. "I appreciate your time in speaking with me. Hopefully, this won't take very long." Depending on what they discovered.

While Liberty led the way to the range's double doors, the suited man who had dropped her off, drove to the side, and parked the golf cart, then trailed them at a distance. Likely, he was one of her security guards.

Liberty showed her into the cool interior. Dark brown walls and gleaming floors shone with a high-polished wood finish. Low glass windows covered half the length from the floor to the ceiling, and a skylight roofing at the middle allowed ample light into the space. It was long, longer than it seemed from outside. Angel slowed her pace and allowed Liberty to walk past her deeper inside. Gun cleaning tables hugged the far walls, and opposite them were stalls marked as Beginner, others Intermediate, and Mastery. Hay was strewn across the floor within each stall, about thirty in all from a quick count. She wondered whether the hay was there as foot padding or as a simulation of natural ground, but didn't ask. Focused, she kept her eyes open. Safety warnings were taped on the wall. The Intermediate and Mastery shooting stalls, marked with yellow and red paint at the edges, were gated with safety warnings taped at the entrances and warnings not to operate a weapon without necessary approval.

Then Angel passed close to a room where a clear glass door revealed enough weaponry for a small army. A quick glance showed antiques and marksman rifles, obviously expensive guns she'd never seen in person before, guns you'd only find in specialty gun stores. She held her tongue until they reached an office at the far end and stepped into an expansive room with a desk, PC, and chairs surrounding it. A lady, sitting at what might be a receptionist desk, rose when the three entered.

"Good morning, Ms. Liberty. Are you ready for your morning practice? I have everything set up in your private practice room." The lady, who seemed to be around fifty years of age, started sitting but straightened again. "Oh, and I had them bring your morning coffee over since you said you had a meeting." The lady threw Angel a quick glance, so Angel dipped her head to acknowledge her.

"Yes. Thank you, Nellie," Liberty responded with authority. "I will let you know if I need anything else. And please hold my calls until we're finished."

Beyond them outside, Angel had spotted a horse stable, hidden away in the back corner of the estate, now visible from the side window. A horse grazed outside it, and Angel wondered how Liberty could maintain all this. There had to be enough people working here to support her.

Liberty spun to Angel and paused. "Would you mind

chatting with me while I practice? I have a flight to catch in about forty minutes, and I both need to chat with you and practice a bit before I leave."

After thinking for a moment, Angel nodded. "Sure." She took out her cell phone, texted Pierce an update, and then followed Liberty. They turned a small corner and entered a separate, larger stall with a door. Several guns rested in a locked case, which Liberty unlocked and removed two, handing one to Angel. "Since you're here, instead of watching, why don't you practice with me while we talk? I'd like to get to know you folks at the SSPD. One of the things I've been told is that you guys are good at everything you do, including shooting. Best me."

Angel accepted the gun, the safety glasses and ear protection, and her challenge. "Well, I'm not here to compete, but a little practice never hurt anyone." With only one stall here, she'd go one round and be done.

She took the time while they got served their rounds by the man who'd followed them, to observe the space. Here, the glass window ran from roof to ceiling, revealing a grand view. The targets were set farther away than the ones she'd seen outside. So she knew. This had to be Liberty's private practice area, further confirmed by the cup of coffee steaming on a table in the right corner.

"I'm here to ask you about Randy like I'd mentioned when we spoke." Angel kicked things off with the primary goal, not letting herself be distracted by the grandiose.

"Yes, I do remember you saying so. What questions do you have?" Liberty stepped aside and allowed Angel to take the first couple of shots. She hit the center and set the weapon and goggles down, keeping the earmuffs secure over her ears, then stepped aside.

Liberty whistled. "Good shot." As she applauded, her slim golden bracelet jingled. "I guess you're as good as they say you people are. I'll make sure not to land on the wrong side of the law, then." Liberty took her former spot and began firing.

So, Angel fired off a set of her own questions, undeterred by the applause. She was here for information to solve a murder case, and solve it she would. "Were you there that night at the high school?"

"I was on a late-night run as I couldn't sleep, so a run felt perfect to clear my head."

"Were you close enough? Did you see something?"

"Not at first. I started my jog at the cafeteria and rounded the bend to the sports complex before the loud voices alerted me that something was up." Liberty fired off a couple more rounds. They all hit their target's center.

"And from the records I was granted access to, both by local police and school archives, you were the only witness who hadn't submitted a report, although you were mentioned a couple of times."

"Odd." She shot a few more rounds, then frowned,

straightened, and set her weapon down. Then she removed her safety goggles. "Is that what they told you?"

"Indirectly, yes." Angel nodded, leaning on the waist-high bulletproof glass partition. "They mentioned not having a report on file, despite indicating you had been there."

"I was there. But I had told them what happened. How Randy's voice drew me to the altercation."

"Apparently, your report was skipped. It has been said that Randy was shouting to David. Did you hear what she said?"

Silent for a moment, Liberty lifted her cup of coffee, added sugar and cream, then stirred it and sipped. The steam had worn off, and Angel wondered whether there was still any warmth left in it. When her host looked up, sadness dimmed her eyes. Then, almost immediately, it was gone. "You know, something about being a victim of assault thrice makes you want to fight the signs anywhere you see it."

Liberty had been assaulted...thrice? "I'm sorry to hear that." Angel cringed. Would her questions raise things the lady would rather not chat about?

"Thank you." A quick nod followed before Liberty set her cup down, folded her arms, and braced against the partition. As her lips pressed tightly, a distance in her eyes appeared as though she was reliving...something unpleasant. "I recall the scream I heard that night. I ran from where I was jogging toward the sound. By the time I arrived, Randy had jumped out of the maintenance space. Yes, I heard what she said."

She faced Angel fully. "She said she was about to be gang-raped. I heard those words and the panic behind them. As a woman, I reacted instantly, and blood pounded in my ears, for her."

A sigh escaped her lips. "I saw the body language of the boys chasing her, and I knew—without a doubt—she was saying the truth. And as soon as those guards flashed their lights, called for backup, and involved the police, you had never seen better-behaved boys before." She shrugged. "Their gang-up against Randy's accusation the following day led me to speak up. I provided my statement to the school authorities who should've given it to the police. I guess my report didn't line up with the official school statement that there had been a misunderstanding. So, they must've tossed it out."

Angel scribbled on her note. "I'm guessing that must be why you got mentioned in the archive notes but not in the police report." She glanced up at Liberty. "Who signed the school report?"

"I'm not sure." Liberty shrugged. "Likely one of the counselors who are typically called in for behavioral matters. One was always available around the clock."

Angel notated that too. "Can I ask why you're so obsessed with guns?" She'd mentally searched for a more politically-correct query, but, finding none, she stuck with her first thought. No celebrity she knew of embraced their love of self-defense and weaponry like Liberty. But Angel wished to hear how much she embraced the love of preserving lives that weren't hers too.

"I'm sure it seems as though I'm addicted to guns and shooting. But the contrary is true. I've supported gun-control legislation for years. I've voted against allowing mentally ill folks, minors, and people in unstable domestic situations access to guns. I support ID, background checks, and criminal record and mental health verification prior to gun sales. And I support the retraction of permits when an individual's safety compliance status changes. After all, there are more than enough guns in the world if we chose to use them strictly for hunting. We don't need to kill. We don't exact justice. That's what the police, you guys, are for." She settled her weapon and Angel's on the counter, and the man took both to secure them.

"So, why amass weapons sufficient to arm an army?" Angel asked straightforwardly.

"Well, first and foremost..." Liberty looked up and smiled, one of the few times she did. "I'm not addicted to guns. Not in the way you think."

She led the way out of the private practice stall. "The main reason I do this is it serves as a place to clear my head while I engage my hands. A place where I can shoot and think without hurting people." They cleared the first room where the assistant had been, though she wasn't on her seat any longer. Angel waited while Liberty left her a note, then rejoined her walking toward the exit. "Another reason, which

I don't publicize, is after the last assault I wished to empower myself. God defends me, but I have to take steps, too, to provide minimal defense the next time someone thinks I'm a piece of something." She paused as they reached the door. "The collection of rare guns began when my acting career took off."

When they stepped outside, Angel paused at the entrance. "Is there anything else you remember about that night? Have you been in touch with any of those boys since or have a relationship with them?"

Liberty shook her head. "I've got no reason to. Two of them are in Hollywood, but I have no interactions with them." She gave a slight pause and inched up an eyebrow. "Matter of fact, one lives twenty miles from here, and I don't think I heard you mention him when we spoke on the phone. Richard Fletcher, a son of old money. I'm not sure what he does for a living, but he was there that night and part of what went on. He stopped by once, but I warned him against coming here again. At the school, I remember that he'd smacked me once. I reported it, and the school authorities did nothing. But he was one of 'the pack' as we called them then, though usually lingering at the fringes of their activities most times, so he went scot-free. I wouldn't let him anywhere near my home. I'm not sure what he was after, but he sure didn't get an audience."

Angel perused her list with a finger and frowned. "You are right. I don't see his name on my list. I'll check once I get back to the office." Did David forget to include him or did he not know about the guy? She extended a card to Liberty. "Thank you very much for your time. If you remember anything else, feel free to give me a call."

A nod followed as Liberty walked back to the golf cart, her security man in tow. "I will. Enjoy the rest of your day. And I hope you nail whoever killed Randy. She'd suffered once before, and she didn't deserve to die."

"I concur." Angel left the estate, feeling even more determined to find and arrest whoever killed Miranda Sow.

21

"WOE TO YOU WHO PLUNDER, THOUGH YOU HAVE NOT BEEN *plundered; And you who deal treacherously, though they have not dealt treacherously with you! When you cease plundering, you will be plundered; when you make an end of dealing treacherously, they will deal treacherously with you."- Isaiah 33:1*

ANGEL ARRIVED AT THE ADDRESS ON FILE FOR RICHARD Fletcher with Pierce. Could this be correct? She cross-checked her notepad. Yes, it was. A frown curved her eyebrows. "This looks like destitution, not old money."

"Same thought here," Pierce said and stroked his beard.

They approached the isolated old house, a crooked roof

framing ivy trailing over corroding redbrick walls. Buckling under nature's intrusion and time's cruelty, how did it even still stand? Although set in an area most people had moved away from, abandoning worn-down houses possessing little to no commercial value, it seemed only this house had smoke rising out of its chimney. Cautious, she motioned to Pierce, who took out his gun, and removed the safety, as did she. When they reached the house, she rapped on the door, held her gun facing down, and waited.

Soon, the door squeaked open, and an elderly lady peered out. "Yes?"

Her brown eyes matched her brown overall coat, a coat seemingly thick enough to serve as a winter coat.

Angel met her gaze and held it. "May we enter?"

The woman eyed Angel. "Not really. Give me a second."

When the woman shut the door, Pierce motioned to Angel. "Going to check the back."

Angel nodded while she waited.

Moments later, the door reopened, and the lady swung it wider. "You can come in now."

Angel stepped in and slowed her steps after entering the cluttered home. Bags of stuff leaned against the corners of the walls, and she trailed a narrow path to the living room. "Does Richard Fletcher live here?"

Almost as soon as the question was out of her lips, Pierce shouted from out back. "We have a runner!"

She jumped over the clutter toward his voice and exited

via the kitchen door. Outside, two men tousled in the grass, struggling for a gun. One of them was Pierce. The other must've been Richard.

Angel ran toward them. Then a gun went off behind her.

"HOLD IT RIGHT THERE, MISSY," THE OLDER WOMAN SAID TO Angel, who aimed her gun right back at her.

"Why would I do so, ma'am?"

The woman held the gun pretty steady for a lady of her age. "I said, hold it right there." She took a few steps forward. "My grandson will not be used again as a scapegoat after what that tramp accused him of, robbing him of a decent life." She shook her head. "And you won't barge in here asking about him for no reason. So, I suggest you and your friend leave." Above her steady aim, her gray eyes peered back at Angel, just as steady, firm, and calm. "Richard won't leave this house. Ever."

"I'll say we're not leaving until we talk to Richard first." Angel waved her gun. "And I suggest you put the gun down before you hurt yourself."

The woman remained where she was.

Stalemate.

Grunts grated her ears from both men fighting for the gun behind her. Angel shifted toward them slightly, but the soft explosion of a shot, and the puff of dust following the gunfire between her legs, stayed her feet. She scowled at the elderly lady. "Ma'am, I am a police officer, and if you try that again, I will be forced to return the favor."

Silence.

"Put your weapon down, ma'am, for the last time."

"I won't. And I suggest you leave my property."

"We have to question your grandson."

"He's done nothing wrong."

"We'll determine that."

"Thank you, but I already did. No one is taking him anywhere."

"Who said anything about taking him somewhere, if he did nothing worth taking somewhere?"

Silence.

"I said, leave." Her hand trembled.

"No," Angel countered.

She winced at the thuds of blows exchanged by both men still locked in a fistfight behind her.

"The last person who came looking for him here, that Randy lady, ask her how it went for her, huh? Then you know how it will be for you. Again, leave before you regret it."

"Grandma? Where are you—" someone said from inside the house, then emerged fully, and gasped as he began reaching for something from behind his jeans.

Angel didn't wait. She shot his thigh before he brandished a weapon. Before his grandma could shoot at her again, she shot the woman's thigh too, and she fell to the ground. Angel rushed toward the lady to kick away the gun when the younger man who'd emerged earlier aimed at her.

She had no choice. She shot him point blank. His face seemed familiar, but she had little time to process it as she seized the woman's gun from the ground, spun, and rushed to support Pierce who was holding down Richard. She threw him some cuffs.

After cuffing Richard, Pierce swiped beads of sweat off his forehead. "Are we clear?"

She nodded. "I think we are unless someone else shows up armed and shooting. Let's call this in."

"What was going on there?" Pierce asked her as they lifted Richard and his grandma to their feet, after being assured SSPD officers were on their way.

Angel shook her head. "I'm not sure. But I guess this lady knows something about how Randy died." She spun to the woman. "And I suggest she starts talking by the time backup arrives."

ANGEL SAT ACROSS FROM THE OLDER WOMAN IN AN INTERVIEW room at the SSPD and could hardly believe what Pierce and she had uncovered.

The lady's cuffs contrasted the character she had played on TV. "Mary Chambers, you played a cop for years. And now you shoot at real cops? And you're a killer?"

The lady was silent, and wiry gray hair fell over her face. Then she leaned forward. "Have you ever seen your only promising grandson's future go to waste because some girl accused him of threatening to harass her in high school? My baby was innocent. They were trying to smear him. He couldn't get into a law enforcement career because of her accusation. Frustrated, he went into drugs. Then the creditors came knocking, and we lost everything." She shook her head. "No, he had to find her. Had to make her pay, but he didn't have the spine for it." Hoarse laughter, unbecoming of the lady she'd portrayed for so many years in front of millions of people, came through her throat. "No way. I was tired of watching him wallow and wither away. So, I sent Collins. He had the heart to do what should have been done many years ago."

Collins was Richard's brother, whom Angel had unfortunately killed. "He killed Randy. You sent him to kill Randy." Her heart wrenched at the conspiratorial nature of this lady.

She spoke through gritted teeth and a burning gaze. "Yes, I did, and I don't regret it. She deserved it for what she did. She ruined our lives." What altered this lady from a beloved character to a criminal?

This wasn't the time to figure that out. Angel had no

other option. Heartbroken at what needed to be done, she proceeded. "Ma'am, I'm placing you under arrest for the murder of Miranda Sow. You have the right to remain silent. Anything you say can and will be used against you in a court of law. You have a right to an attorney...."

As Angel read her her rights, the lady laughed hard, with pain written over her eyes. Angel wished she could help the lady heal, but it wasn't part of her job so she relented and whispered a prayer instead. Then an officer cuffed her and led her away, but it seemed she yet had one more thing to say as she paused briefly at the door. She pinned Angel with a gaze. "If you charge me, you have unleashed a storm. You won't live through it, I promise you. You might not even make it home. I suggest you release me without charges."

Angel leaned across from the table, unwilling to bow to any threats, even from people she pitied. "We shall see."

"PIERCE, TELL ME WHAT YOU GOT." ANGEL RETURNED TO HER office and hovered behind her chair, gripping it with a hand.

He flicked on her screen, took her chair, and revealed what he'd been working on. "Okay, while you were interviewing the suspect, I was digging, and I found something interesting."

"Spill it." Angel sat and rolled her chair closer to the PC.

"Their family was on the straight and narrow until something happened twenty years ago, inducing the woman to leave her acting career. Then, not long afterward, her husband divorced her. A few years after the divorce, her grandchildren moved home. And their wealth began dwindling. They got involved with some people who were suspected of dealing drugs largescale. And in the process, the grandkids became addicts. Little by little, they withered away their family fortune and were left with debt. Then, I suspect, the blackmail started. They made large payments to groups founded by local gang leaders and got roped into their circle. Richard's wife is a daughter of the leading local gang icon. It's a web. Another surprise? Richard and Danielson, the congressional candidate, are cousins. And he has a business partnership with some members of the gang. We have a whole situation that simply unraveled here."

"Wow." Angel curled her arms. "I guess Miranda was caught between powerful, rich, and determined enemies." The woman's threats began to make sense.

"And, get this, the deceased brother of Richard, a truck driver, owns a black Tundra."

Both her eyes rounded.

"And he frequents the roads serving the valley road area for water delivery, they say."

"He must've been delivering more than water."

"I concur." Pierce nodded. "But, since he knew the route well, it makes sense he'd be the perfect person they'd send to take out Randy."

"Well, let's check his truck for any damages and go from there," Angel said as the captain walked in.

But she still had one more question bugging her. "Why do you think the grandma confessed so easily? I'd expected some resistance."

Pierce shifted and faced her. "Because the minute we knocked on her door, we had them. It would've only been a matter of matching traffic cameras from the accident, running the Tundra's registration to her grandson, Collins. And the rest would've fallen into place. It was game over."

Angel rubbed the goose bumps on her skin. "It's just so sad. I liked her TV character."

Pierce turned up a lip. "Me too. Does it matter that her ex-husband was a cop, they'd had an ugly divorce, and he'd left her and married a fellow cop?" Angel shrugged, not sure what to say, and let Pierce finish his thoughts. "But people change, you know."

"That they do," she concurred. "I can understand how those set of facts could make someone bitter, but she shouldn't kill because of it. Like you said, people change."

"Great job, you two." The captain shook their hands.

"Thank you, sir." Angel shifted. "And I need to ask a favor."

"Anything."

"Pierce and I will need police protection for the near future."

"Oh, I watched your interview. Good job there too." Then

his smile flattened into a hard line. "And your request is granted. No one threatens one of my people without facing consequences. We'll put the necessary equipment and staff in place." He patted her back and left.

Pierce spun. "Why do we need protection?"

She moved closer. "I'll fill you in."

22

~

Violet sat in the hospital waiting room, clasped her hands, and settled both between her knees. She lowered her head and tried to make sense of the past twenty-four hours while doctors fought to save Tim's life. Tim, basically trekking from Mexico to avoid getting killed. Her, caught in her brother's crosshairs, and this cop, who showed up out of nowhere and dove headfirst into her life, company, and situation. She clasped her head between her hands. "Oh, dear Lord, this is not happening." She pressed urgent hands on her eyes, hoping to stave off the sleep forcing its way in. It had been a few hours since Tim came out of surgery. Although it had gone well, the doctors weren't sure when he would wake up. That had been the issue.

Yawning, she saw someone approach, and she turned fully, then stood. It was the cop, Mike. "Hey. How's Tim?"

Mike wore an unreadable expression. "He's stable for now, but he's in a coma. Doctors say it could be a while..."

Her heart tightened, but she managed a nod. "I understand, but I don't like it. Not one bit. Tim shouldn't get shot for me."

Mike took her arm, and gently guided her to a pair of seats. He squatted in front of her and looked her in the eye. "I don't want you to blame yourself. This isn't your fault. Yes, it may have started because of what you own, but you are not to take responsibility. Someone tried to kill your friend and possibly chased him all the way from Mexico. The license plate of the vehicle in question was grabbed by a security camera, and we traced it to a car rental facility in Arizona. We found the individual who was named as the car renter, but they'd fled to Mexico. We have a team headed there now. With assistance from the Mexican Police force with jurisdiction, we will find them, and we will protect you." He touched her arm. "You are not to blame."

The sound of a baby crying drew her eyes away for a moment. Then she focused back on him.

"Do you believe me?" As his gaze roamed her face, she

saw how clear his eyes were, brimming with determination for protection and for justice, and she nodded.

"Yes, and thank you."

He squeezed her hand, and it rolled some of her worry away. "My men will escort you home and stay watch around your home overnight, but since they thought Tim was the owner of the poem, I believe you might be safe, for now." He released her hand.

"What happens when Tim wakes up? If they know he's still alive, they could still come after him." She looked away, wondering how the nearness of a man she hardly knew could affect her when she wasn't even thinking about it. "I want to make sure Tim stays safe—for good."

"We can explore options when he wakes up, depending on whether he is still being targeted." Mike straightened.

Did he see her reaction earlier? Was that why he'd straightened? She couldn't tell.

"Options like?" she pressed.

He trailed his mustache with a finger, lost in thought, and blinked—oblivious to her swallowing hard at the gesture. This was not the time to think about Mike's handsomeness, but she couldn't deny being drawn to the man. However, she disciplined her mind to focus on Tim. "Depending on the threat level, if the worst comes to worst, we could issue a death certificate and, with his consent, change Tim's name and identity."

"Um, okay. That sounds extreme."

Mike scratched his head. "I know. Sometimes, extreme measures are necessary to save lives. He can continue his life, but he won't officially be in the witness protection program. It can be done."

"Is there an option that won't involve something so drastic?"

"Since we're so close to nabbing the suspect, I believe we won't go that far. But if it came to it, yes, we would consider granting Tim a new identity." Mike rubbed his chin for a moment. "How safe would you like him to be?"

She got his point, but she would have a hard time accepting a name change if she were in Tim's shoes. "Will I be notified of his new identity, if things get to that?" She prayed that it didn't and the team would be successful in catching the suspect or suspects.

"I'm sure he will tell you, but it will solely be Tim's decision about who to share such information with."

"I understand." She nodded. "Will he move to another city or state, if that should happen?"

"Possibly. When we encounter such aggression and an international threat, we take very good precautions to protect our people. Also, remember we don't yet know the culprits behind this. It's even more imperative we protect Tim's identity until we're sure he's totally safe." Mike glanced down the hall. "If he doesn't wake up soon, and we need to reach a decision about his future, we will get in touch with his family."

"He only has a living grandma, and she lives in a nursing home. I can provide you her information if you need it. Tim gave it to me, just in case."

"He trusts you." Mike watched her beneath a measured gaze. "You both are quite close."

Was that some spark of interest in his eye? She tilted her chin. "Yes, we are. He's my prayer partner and my friend." When he said nothing, she added, "And no, we're not in a romantic relationship, if you were wondering."

"Oh." His shoulders slackened.

Was he interested in her? She wasn't sure and didn't want to ask as her mind was occupied with ensuring Tim's safety. She blamed herself for suggesting she and Mike fake-date just to protect her from Pete. Maybe that was why she was seeing him in a different light than simply a cop. But it was all she could come up with on the short term considering she was trying to protect him and herself too.

Her heart longed to see Tim smile again. To see him laugh and to see him live. "Is there a time frame for when we get another update about Tim?"

Mike turned to glance at the clock on the wall. A dark stain smeared the back of his shirt.

Violet gasped. "You're bleeding. A doctor should check you out."

He twisted, then flexed his shoulders. "It's got to be some grazing. I had thought I bumped something there. Sure, I'll go down to the ER to get it treated." He took out a notepad.

"I'm going to ask for you to give me your phone number, email address, home address, and other identifying information. If we need to reach you in an emergency, I want to have multiple options, especially due to The New Rulebook case. My captain will send someone to watch Tim while I report to the station to update our team."

Mike scratched his chin covered by a neatly-trimmed beard. "Although it would've been best to have you come with me to see the captain, since he might have questions, and to provide a report on your suspicions with the case on Pete, I decided against it for safety reasons to ensure your brother suspects nothing. Until we hear back from the team en route to Mexico, working with the Mexican law enforcement authorities for this case, everyone stays put. Meanwhile, I suggest you go home and get some sleep."

She shook her head. "I'm not going anywhere. Not until Tim has woken up."

Mike frowned. "I understand your concerns, but you do need to sleep. You've virtually been in this hospital, waiting, for almost a day now. You need some rest if you can be useful to Tim when he wakes up. And don't you have to go to work tomorrow? If you're gone for too long, Pete may suspect something, and we don't want that to happen. You can always call to check on him. And you can spend your evening here, after work, to sit with him. Maybe talk to him so he can hear a familiar voice. I was told people in a coma can hear you, and I tend to believe there could be some truth to it."

"Thanks, Mike, but I'm staying. At least for another day. I'll call Pete and let him know Tim is sick and in the hospital and I'm staying here. Nothing more. That should buy me twenty-four more nonsuspicious hours to monitor Tim's progress and to pray for his recovery." Unsure whether the man was a Christian or understood the power of prayer, she openly shared her intentions.

That seemed to catch his attention as he drew closer. "Oh." He blinked. "You'll pray? Are you a Christian?"

She nodded. "Yes, am."

"Me too. I'll pray for your friend." He observed her with that...look...again. "And for you too. See you in a few hours then. If anything happens," he pulled out a card from his wallet and handed it to her, "call me on any of these numbers."

She took the card, then gave him hers, thankful that the hospital had given her scrubs to change into after she washed Tim's blood off her hands and body. She'd gone to the gift shop, bought a brown T-shirt and black slacks, and changed. As she waited, she'd prayed and dozed off. Tim's surgery had lasted for hours, but the time passed quickly as she remained deep in prayers for him. "I'll see you later."

As Mike's shadow disappeared from the outer doors, she lowered her head to pray for Tim and, for herself, and for Mike—who was making small inroads into her heart.

～

Two days later, as soon as Violet left work, she headed to the hospital. She parked, walked past a departing ambulance that seemed like it had dropped off an emergency patient, took a left turn, and she spun toward the healing garden at the center. The greenery of the healing garden made the hospital seem less stiff and unwelcoming.

Striding past long-stay patients sitting on the benches while taking in some fresh evening air beneath early-budding cherry trees, she used the walkway to climb to the first floor, then caught the elevator to Tim's room.

After arriving in his room and having watched Tim until it was dark, she decided she needed to go to church and pray. A heavy burden weighed on her heart. So much was hanging in the balance, and she felt a need for a place of complete openness with God.

She turned to Mike, who stood briefing an officer who had arrived to watch Tim's room. Mike had faithfully been here every day, and they'd talked for hours before he would leave. They shared their interests, favorite sport teams, favorite Scriptures, and life experiences. They laughed together, shared meals to save themselves trips to the hospital cafeteria, and grew much closer. She felt like she knew the man well enough, even though it had only been a few days since their first chance meeting. "Mike?"

He glanced at her, raised a finger to request her patience, wrapped up with the officer, and came over. "Yes?"

"I need to go to the church and pray. I can't figure all this out on my own. I need some time with God. So please let me know if Tim wakes up while I'm there."

He was silent. Then he peered in her face with kind eyes. "Mind if I join you? I mean, with all that has happened, I could use some prayer time myself. It's been so busy at the station, tracking the team in Mexico... I haven't had time to pray either. And I was going to let you know that with help from the Mexican authorities, they've nabbed the driver."

Her eyes widened. "Really? Great." Some relief swept through her, and her shoulders slacked. "Did he say why he targeted Tim?"

"He didn't talk, but his collaborator did. She spilled everything, including who paid them. A group which specializes in relics paid them to do away with Tim."

Violet pressed a hand on her heart. "Why?"

Mike scratched his head. "Well, they had thought he had some gold stored somewhere since he was singing about kings, so it was apparently a robbery."

"A robbery?"

"Yes, but that's not the interesting part."

"What else?" Violet leaned on the wall as he faced her fully.

"She says she heard one of the group's members sing your dad's poem as a song in Spanish. When she asked, he said it was a folklore song within his local community. Apparently, digging deeper, it originated from travelers said to have had a former king from a Spanish island kingdom called Lanzarote, passing through the area some hundreds of years ago. Although, as the story went, there was no difference among the travelers, and no one could identify the king among them. He said that was what old folks in their place had told them growing up. As years went by, people feigned to be descendants of that king, but it was never proven true. The song was more in tribute to them because the traveling group had been armed but didn't attack them, so they sang their praises long after the travelers moved on."

Violet was gaping by then. "Huh. How come I've never heard this before? That's interesting."

Mike nodded. "It sure is. But that wasn't the direction of our investigation so we focused on our reason for being there —we nabbed the guys, and they sent a confirmation that Tim was dead. A photo of some random person who looked a little like him. We're hoping that satisfies their contractor's bloodthirst. I thought you might want to know the story, though."

"Goodness." She let out a whoosh. "An attempted robbery caused an international chase? I'm so glad he's safe now. At least, for as long as they believe the tale."

"You could find out more about the story and the said king if you like...." He studied her again.

Violet shook her head and waved the suggestion off. "Not while Tim is here fighting for his life, no. I think I've learned enough. I'm going to leave the past right where it is, and I'm sure Tim would say the same. But thanks for your readiness to support me."

"You're welcome." A brief smile warmed his face. "Sadly, we had to let the woman go free for cooperating. She said their job was finished, and the other fellow had been arrested. That was what she communicated to them. And she promised never to come after Tim or to enter the US again. We, and the Mexican law enforcement folks, already have a watch placed on her ID in case she changes her mind. So, for now, Tim is safe and can continue his life."

"Thanks, Mike." She hugged him. "This is the best news I could've heard right now."

"Thank God. We hope you can have some rest now, save for Pete." He glanced at a second officer who joined Tim's security watch. Mike waved at him, and he waved back, then went to speak to the officer already posted. While Violet thanked God in her heart, Mike returned his attention to her. "I'm off for a couple of hours, and I know I won't sleep so I'd rather pray. Then I'll head to the station to see what I can find out. My partner is already investigating the information you provided about The New Rulebook."

Not seeing any reason to refuse, Violet smiled. "Sure. You can come. But I should warn you, I don't pretend when I pray. With the way I'm feeling right now, my prayers can get intense."

He chuckled. "Suits my present mood too. I have both a heavy heart and weighted shoulders I need to lean on God for as this case with Pete keeps unraveling. New layers are uncovered every day, and I need godly direction and prayer. I'd rather do it with someone who wouldn't mind my intensity either."

Violet shrugged. "Fine. Let's go." She led the way out of the hospital, joined him in his police cruiser at his offer, and off they went to Christ Believers Church.

23

"In this the love of God was manifested toward us, that God has sent His only begotten Son into the world, that we might live through Him." -1 John 4:9

～

Upon reaching the church, Violet led the way inside, and Mike followed to the front and settled into a pew. She spun to him and spoke in low tones as they were alone. In the wee hours, everywhere was quiet. "Please feel free to take any seat you like. And to pray however you like. I'm not sure when I'll be done praying, but I'll take a taxi home so don't feel like you need to wait for me."

He nodded. "Sure." He made his way over to the altar and wiped his palms on the sides of his pants. Then kicking off his shoes, he sat on a lower step and unbuckled his weapon belt, setting it down beside him. He leaned on a step and curled his arms around his knees. Then his lips moved in prayer.

Violet knelt down, disciplined her mind, and focused on her own prayer. Bowing her head, she thought about the chase, the shooting, Tim's injury, his surgery, and Pete. Violet tried to speak, but her heart felt fuller than her mouth. How could she verbalize how she was feeling? So much had happened, even in the last couple of hours, that it sapped her of words. So, she took her favorite form of prayer when words failed—whispering to Him where it hurts—and praying in tongues. *Thank You, Lord, for stopping the people who were after Tim. I'm grateful to You.*

She swallowed hard as the image of Tim lying in the hospital bed for days now in a coma, appearing vulnerable, yet surrounded by a strange sense of peace, overwhelmed her. She choked on a tear when she thought of how close he came to dying. *Thank You, my Father, for not allowing the enemy steal Tim from us. I'm grateful. Oh that he would wake now....*

Her mind moved over to Pete, and she could seldom breathe for the burden in her heart weighed so heavy. There was so much to communicate. No words seemed good enough, so her heart did the talking in groanings.

How much time had passed before she peeled her tear-filled eyes open when she heard a crinkling sound, she had no idea. Mike had his head bowed to the ground at the base of the podium of the altar, and the image stamped itself into her soul. But her heart was still heavy for Pete so it returned to praying for her only brother. Right now, she recognized that, in order not to be crushed under the pressure she felt regarding Pete's sharp behavior changes, she needed to pour some of these thoughts and feelings into words. She gripped the chilly curve of the chair in front of her.

"Dear Lord, I'm not sure how to begin, but I'm here before You, laying out my heart openly without fear. You have never failed me. You won't start now."

She lifted her gaze skyward and shook her head. *Do I have the courage to spill these painful words wrapped around my soul for so long they feel as though they were a part of it?*

Violet wasn't sure she knew how, but for her own sake, she had to try. She couldn't just give up. She had to pray and seek the face of the Lord. "Lord, I'm trying to understand why my life is changing at a rapid-fire pace while my brother's life is going the opposite direction." Feeling tears coming, she let them escape. As they trickled down her cheeks, she prayed more. "Lord, it's been many years since Pete served You. Every time I broach the subject, he turns against me. He doesn't go to church. He doesn't seek You. He doesn't revere You. He doesn't have the fear of God in his heart."

She crouched lower on her knees. "And that is the main reason his recent changes bother me. If I can only understand what's going on with Pete, then maybe I can help him."

Violet prayed on until she felt Scripture impressed on her heart—"the battle is not yours. It is the Lord's."

Frustration crept up her heart because all she wanted to hear from God was that, yes, she could do something to change Pete. Or to turn him from the direction he was going, so she pushed back in prayer. "Lord Jesus, I love my brother, and I want him to be saved. I want him to do the right thing. I want Pete to make the right decisions. I don't want to lose my brother. Please change him through me." Yes, it sounded selfish, but she said what she wanted regardless. There were no pretenses between her and God.

Again, the Words overrode hers in her heart—"the battle is the Lord's, not yours."

Frustrated, Violet stood, moved to the altar, and sat in the center of the dais. When she'd walked past Mike, she heard him groaning in prayer. With his head lifted and tears flowing down his cheeks, she wondered about his anguish. But she had her own praying to complete so she faced the other way. Nevertheless, something struck her about his vulnerability, displayed without care for who heard or saw him, even when he knew she was there. So absorbed in prayer, Mike was completely focused on the Lord and not on anyone else.

She turned her back to him, folded her arms between her thighs, and lifted her gaze to heaven once more. This time, sure she was more exhausted by the response she was getting, than by being physically tired, Violet persevered in prayer. Something had to change. Something had to give. She was tired of making the same petition over and again for a stubborn brother who refused Christ and hoarded enough secrets to create a confidential cabinet.

Yes, she could make God change His mind about this. He could save her brother now. No, He wouldn't let Pete be lost forever.

The thought of Pete going to hell sent a shudder through her, and she pressed her eyes closed. "Lord, You are good. I don't want to see my brother grow worse. He has become distant and more cold-hearted. I want to see Pete saved, please," she cried her deepest prayer. "I don't want my brother to go to hell. I want Pete to make heaven," she groaned the prayer in her spirit, and sobs swallowed her speech. "I don't want to lose him. I don't want him to commit a crime and go to jail. I don't want him to kill again, if he did before. Please, Lord, help me. Save him now."

And for the third time, she heard those words again —"the battle is the Lord's and not yours."

Violet buried her head into her hands and wept until her eyes throbbed. When she finished laying her burdens at the Lord's feet, relief worked through her. If this was God's will for her not to press further about Pete, she would relinquish him to God. Little by little, in her heart, she gave everything Pete had done to her, over to God. Violet allowed the Word she had received to comfort her instead of frustrate her.

She accepted that, as much as she wanted what she

wanted, God knew what He was doing. "Lord, please take over. I accept to release this battle to Your able hands. I've fought it long enough and have realized how incapable I am for it. So, take this. Take over Pete, and let Your Righteous will be done." Peace flooded her soul. She sang one song of worship in a low tone. Then, as soon as she felt a release in her spirit, she simply sat there, soaking in the Lord's surrounding presence.

"Hey." Mike tapped her shoulder, and she turned. "May I join you?"

She nodded with eyes as puffy as his. "Sure. Please sit." She scooted over, even though the podium of the altar was large enough for them and more. "Are you done praying?"

He sniffed. "Yes, for now. Do we ever finish?"

Violet found herself chuckling. "No, we don't." She glanced at him as he crossed his arms around his knees.

The light at the altar shone on him and revealed his chiseled jaw and the curve of his trimmed hair above his neck. She couldn't deny that this man was handsome. "Were you praying for your family?"

He stared at her for a moment. "I have no family," his Adam's apple bobbed, "at least, none that will consider me their family—thanks to something I did in my past. I've learned the hard way that, sometimes, those who are closest to you are the hardest to offer you forgiveness."

She settled a hand on his arm. "I'm sorry to hear that."

He covered her hand with his own, and a smile softened

his features. "It's okay. Let's just say I have an older brother who treats me sort of like yours treats you. We have that in common, so I understand how you are feeling."

She gulped. "It's harder when they are not saved. I love my brother, but..." She let her voice trail off.

He settled his arms on the floor behind him to support his weight. "Yes, it definitely is. You pray, and you want them saved, like right this minute. But it doesn't happen immediately because their will is involved. God wants everyone saved, but He won't force anyone to accept the gift of salvation. It's a free, fully-paid-for gift. But you have to want it. The process of creating that want is what causes the delay, bringing your will in alignment with God's will." He twisted toward her and offered a sad smile. "The more stubborn your sibling is, the longer the conviction journey. But every prayer of salvation is a seed on the altar, and they will accumulate and bear fruit one day."

Amazed at his wisdom and patience—patience which she didn't readily feel—Violet placed a hand under her jaw and kneeled her elbow on her thigh. "I know. I just...want it to happen now." Her eyes pleaded with his. "Before he gets worse and does something that can land him in jail." She shook her head. "He's too smart to be wasted. I want to see Pete saved." She sighed. "But, then again, who am I to dictate to God? His time is the best."

"Stop putting so much pressure on yourself, Violet. You can't make it happen by your own power." Mike reached out and placed a tentative arm around her shoulder loosely. She knew he was maintaining a respectful distance and appreciated the gesture. "I wished the same for my own brother for a long time. Then I realized that, in addition to being a valid witness for Jesus, sometimes, you just need to keep praying. Trouble is best avoided, but certain people will only see their need for Christ when *in* trouble, not out of it. I'll pray along with you, but I'll still do my job as a police officer where Pete is concerned. Will that be an issue?"

She shook her head again. "Of course not." His hand slid off her shoulder and returned to his thigh. "You have to do your job. I get it. I just wished it didn't have to be my brother at the center of it."

Mike rose and checked his watch. "Wow. It's almost two a.m." He helped her with a hand to get to her feet, and she dusted off the back of her pants as they made their way to where she'd left her purse after he clicked on his weapon belt. "Do you care for some food? I saw an IHOP on our way here, and if it's not too early to have breakfast, I'd like to buy you some food. I'm hungry too, and I'll be heading to the station after dropping you off at the hospital to get your car."

"Sure, breakfast sounds good. Though I've never had it this early, I feel hungry, so let's go." She seized the strap of her purse and slung it over her shoulder.

Mike winked at her, and her belly responded with butterflies. "Moreover, let's not forget you owe me a promised date."

Violet felt her brows curve upward. "I do?"

"Yup." He nodded and grinned. "From the train."

Then she remembered and laughed. "Oh, you know that was fake, for security reasons."

He swept her an admiring glance, sweeping color to her cheeks. "Not to me. Please, lead the way."

As she climbed into the vehicle and Mike drove them, she recalled something her pastor had shared during a special singles' meeting. She could almost quote it word for word.

Anyone, who can kneel with you before God, will stand with you before men. The place of prayer was a place of intimacy with God. And anyone who entered there with her and showed her their true face—vulnerable, unraveled, and with no self-pride—was worth taking a chance at love with. Mike was worth taking a chance with. "This is about the riskiest thing I've ever done, but let's make it a date then. A two-a.m. date."

Mike paused at the stop sign and lifted his eyes upward. "Thank You, Jesus, for answered prayers. Number one down, three more to go."

His eyes met hers, and they both laughed for a change. His eyes sparkled, and she wondered if her acceptance put the glint there. "I will give almost anything to know what the other three prayer points are."

"I'll spill it all on our date."

That sealed the deal.

24

"Great peace have those who love Your law, and nothing causes them to stumble." *–Psalm 119:165*

❧

Violet returned to work two days later and found herself struggling to focus. Her mind kept shifting toward Tim at the hospital until she finally called and checked on him twice before lunch. According to the nurses, he was still in a coma, and at this point, it was expected to last possibly for weeks.

Weighed down, she remembered how he seemed so peaceful the previous day as his chest rose and fell with steady breaths. His dark hair slid to the side of his face like a shield, his pallid skin giving the only indication of his suffering. As she'd stayed by his bedside after her early-morning breakfast-turned-date with Mike, she was amazed by how close the bullet had come to Tim's heart. Doctors said it was a miracle that he'd been alive. She thanked God for saving Tim's life because she wasn't sure what she would do had he lost his life on her account.

Thankfully, those who were pursuing him had disappeared. She longed for him to wake so she could tell him he was safe now.

She glanced at her PC and told herself the truth—she wasn't going to get any work done. The best option was for her to go back to the hospital. She informed Pete of her whereabouts and took off.

~

ANGEL WAS AT THE STATION WHEN THE PHONE CALL CAME. John called her, and the moment she heard the tone of his voice, she knew something was wrong. "John?"

"Angel, I just heard from the pastor that Tim's in the hospital. He was shot, and had surgery at Silver Stone General."

Angel gasped. "I spoke to Tim last week. He can't be shot. He's in Mexico." She and Tim had grown closer after their first date weeks ago and were maintaining a long-distance relationship. They got to chat whenever she could spare the time, and they would be on the phone for hours.

"He was. But, from the information the police provided, things became dangerous with something he was working on in Mexico last week, and he returned unexpectedly," John said.

Was that why he hadn't replied to her calls? She'd gotten his voicemail and thought he was simply busy, though he'd usually called back within a day.

John continued, "He had barely arrived when he was shot in police custody near his home. I don't understand all the details, but since you're one of them, you can ask more questions internally. I wanted to let you know before I head over there. I'm so sorry."

So was she, for whoever attacked the man she loved. Tim had declared his love to her barely three weeks ago, and now someone was trying to snatch him from life? No way. Not if she could do something about it.

"Thanks for calling, John. I'll find out what I can, then head to the hospital soon."

"Sure. I'll meet you there." Then John hung up.

VIOLET SAT AT THE EDGE OF TIM'S BED AND LIFTED HER GAZE as the door opened. "Hi," she greeted the man and woman who entered. The lady was in police uniform, while the man had crusted cement around the ankles of his rugged jeans. His hair was short, and his eyes were sharp.

"Hello," the lady replied, but her gaze settled on Tim as she moved toward him. Only when she drew close enough did Violet see her nametag—Officer Martinez? Where did she know...? "You're Angel." Violet smiled wider. Angel was in a relationship with Tim. "Tim told me about you. We're close friends."

"I am." Angel studied Violet's face. "You must be Violet, then." She reached out a hand, and a faint smile creased her lips.

She bobbed her head. "Yes. And it's a pleasure to finally meet you."

"The pleasure is mine as well. This is my brother, John."

Violet shook hands with John. "Nice to meet you, John."

"Same here." He gave a nod.

"What happened to Tim? I barely had enough time to get the details before I left the station." Angel grasped one of his bedrails and leaned over. "I just needed to see him."

"I understand." Violet gave her a summary of the events and the shooting.

"My goodness." Angel's gaze narrowed. "Do you know who might be after Tim? Any enemies of your family?"

"Besides my brother, Pete? No, I don't. Moreover, Pete wasn't close with our dad and has never cared about the poem or any family history. He has only one obsession now, and I'm the only person standing between him and it. I'm glad, though, that the culprits were caught and dealt with and that Tim is safe."

Angel exhaled, and her shoulders slacked. "Me too, Violet. Sounds like you're going through a rough time." Angel's voice softened. "If you need a sister, I'm here for you."

Warmth spread through Violet's chest. How special to have the instant connection of a sister in Christ—especially when her one sibling was... "Thank you. I appreciate that." She pointed at Tim. "In the meantime, I'm praying our friend will wake up soon."

"Amen to that." John stepped forward, his heavy boots thudding on the slick linoleum.

"Amen," Angel echoed and grabbed a seat. But John leaned against the wall. And the wait continued.

ONE MONTH LATER, VIOLET LEFT HER OFFICE AND DROVE TO the church. Tim still hadn't woken up. She entered the Christ Believers Church again with a heavy heart and sat on the first seat, pulled down more by weariness than by gravity. She sunk her purse into the next chair and lowered her head onto the backrest before her. Glancing at the cross at the altar, she blinked and closed her eyes. "My life is a mess, Jesus. And I'm going to tell you all about it." So she let go of trying to have it together and poured it all on Him.

"It's been one month, five days, and fifteen hours, Lord." She exhaled long and massaged her stiff neck. Working hard for twelve hours a day, six days a week had taken down her health. But that wasn't why she was here today. She continued her prayer, stifling a yawn. "Tim has been in a coma, under police protection, and we don't know if or when he will wake. It's taking too long." She slid to her knees and leaned her shoulder against a church pew.

"I have completed The New Rulebook design." She paused. "And tested to be sure its destruction worked as it should. Everything is set," she added, feeling a pang of guilt, pain, peace, and confusion all at once. "I'm not sure what to do. Pete knows I'm hiding something. I'm in love with Mike, and I'm not even sure how it happened." Laughter escaped her throat. "Pete could kill him if he sees him and knows what Mike and I are up to regarding his pet project." Another sigh followed. "Everything is so complicated now."

She rose to her feet, made her way to the altar, and fell on her knees once more. Sobs racked her body as the words poured out of her. "I'm alone, and I'm fighting Pete on my own. Many times, I want to end the duel, but I can't when I think about how much harm that will cause."

Tears streamed down her cheeks and matted stray hair to her face. "Today, I nearly got caught sneaking the journal out to the car had that young lady not shown up. Had I not been worried about Tim, I likely would have remembered to add the die holding my last ten-percent secret before now, and not have had to bring the journal from home. I'm not sure where to go from here. Pete knows the project is completed and will seek to activate it soon. How can I stop him?"

She peeled open passages in her Bible, and even though she was as tired as ever, she prayed. Prayed for Tim's recovery, prayed for Pete's change of heart. Prayed for The New Rulebook's scheme to be successfully overturned. Prayed about her feelings for Mike. Prayed for Cortexe Corp. Then, again for Pete. She sobbed so hard that, after what felt like an eternity, she grew limp, laid down there, and soon, fell asleep.

Soft sky-blue light glowed in her vision, and Violet saw herself standing where she'd been lying down. She felt swept off her feet and light as air, even though she still stood in a place she didn't readily recognize. Shining light surrounded her but didn't hurt her eyes.

Then across, feet glowed like the sun. "Violet," a Voice said. "Do not be afraid. I have heard your prayer and the gentle whispers of your heart—whispers that traveled straight from your heart to Mine. Well done, daughter. Your crown is waiting, and Pete shall be saved. Give the journal to whom I will show you. Then have My peace." The light faded away.

A sharp chill swept over her skin, and shivering, she jerked awake.

Again, she was lying down at the church altar, and silence surrounded her. She blinked, her heart thudding. Crawling away from there to her feet, she shuddered and wrapped her arms around herself. What just happened? God actually spoke—to *her*? She rehearsed the message, dwelling on every word.

Then realization dawned, and she bowed herself and wept.

Violet inched her face upward and let out the words she already knew the answers to. "Lord Jesus, are You saying what I think You're saying?" She choked out her next words in a gentle, painful whisper. "Is my time on earth done? Am I coming home?"

A quiet certainty settled on her heart. Yes. It was time.

She tried to accept God's will, but her heart wouldn't let her. "Lord, I want to see Pete saved. I've prayed for so long. So did Mom. It cannot happen in my absence. No, Lord! Please. Let me see it happen." She pounded her fist on a step of the altar's podium repeatedly until it throbbed while she sobbed louder.

Pete shall be saved, Violet, a Voice whispered in her heart.

She bowed lower, her shoulders shook harder, and her hair poured over her face and mingled with tears and every kind of fluid. She gripped the altar's edge and shook it hard. It took a while, but little by little, she considered a choice to accept God's will and her possible exit.

She pressed a finger to her throbbing lips. "I love Mike, Lord. I'd hoped to marry him if he asked me to." She rocked her feet dangling loosely off the first step, her faith and trust in God being stretched to snapping. Could she really accept this if it was His will?

That was what trust came down to. She shut her eyes, inhaled deeply. Then she exhaled until she had calmed sufficiently. "Thank You, Lord, for the heads-up." She swallowed and chose to forgive everyone who had offended her whom she might not have already forgiven. "Lord Jesus, I accept whatever is coming, if it is in Your perfect will."

Do not fear those who can hurt the body, but not your soul.

The Lord was so close to her, so close His Words were now physically audible. She'd just had the most vivid vision since she became a born-again Christian. Her spiritual senses were sharper than they'd ever been. She wobbled on her feet, still feeling like she floated.

What was happening? Violet bent her head between her thighs and wept bitterly as the thought of what may be coming swept over her afresh. "Please take care of my honey, Lord. If I must go, find Mike a woman who will love him better than I ever could. Make him happy, and please get him to heaven." With teary eyes, she looked skyward. "Because I'm not saying goodbye to him. I must see Mike in heaven."

Just then, her phone rang, and she walked away from the altar to go get it. She wiped her tears and managed to reach it before it cut off. "Hello?"

"Hi, this is to inform you that your prescription order is ready for pick up," a pleasant automated voice informed.

"Yes..." She opened her mouth to respond. But the church doors swung wide open, and familiar faces stared at her.

"Miss Zendel?"

She said nothing as the phone dropped from her hand

and hit the floor. "Come with us, please. It's urgent." Pete's security guards, fully armed, stopped where she stood. Then they led her by the hand.

She shook off their hands and squared her shoulders. "Why?"

"You withheld company resources, unauthorized, and inconsistencies in your sign-ins in the lab's signature log today showed you left at unapproved times and likely in possession of restricted company property. Therefore, you are required to return to our site immediately to be questioned."

She froze, knowing she couldn't lie and say she didn't do any of those. But she also couldn't say that she did them for a good cause. Not to these guys. Of course, their response had been carefully worded for them by Pete. He was seeking to get his hands on the piece she withheld from The New Rule-book software. The 10 percent she'd withheld. And she would never give it to him.

It was no use calling the police. If she did, Pete's guards would rough-handle her before they arrived. And there was no guarantee they wouldn't kill her before then—and possibly endanger Mike—a chance she wasn't willing to take. Someone had to be alive to take down The New Rulebook. And if it wasn't her, she would find someone who would. But for now, she had to see Pete, face to face. Enough of these go-betweens.

So, armed with quiet determination, she lifted her purse,

slung it over her shoulder, and faced the altar again. *Lord Jesus, You said You hear the whispers of my heart. So, here's one more. Thank You again for not letting me get blindsided. I'm not looking forward to whatever will happen, but thank You for promising to save Pete. I'm grateful.*

Casting one backward glance to the altar from the door, and recalling the vision she'd had minutes earlier, she strode with heavy steps out of the church.

25

"*I KNOW YOUR WORKS, LOVE, SERVICE, FAITH, AND YOUR PATIENCE;* *and as for your works, the last are more than the first.*" –*Revelation 2:19*

VIOLET SAT CROSS-LEGGED AS SHE WAITED FOR PETE INSIDE the Cortexe Corp. complex without access to her phone. The bodyguards had led her into a secure room on the ground floor and waited for her brother to join them to determine her fate. She admitted to no accusation they threw at her and simply insisted that she speak with Pete directly.

She'd spotted increased activity at the complex as they drove her in. Limousines were parked out front as soon as she stepped out. Curious about what was going on, she'd been too tired to ask. Moreover, they quickly ushered her into the room where she now waited, giving her no chance to socialize, leaving her tired, hungry, and thirsty. "Can I have some water, please? Also, if you have a sandwich or something, I'll appreciate it."

One of the bodyguards took steps to an adjacent room, then returned with a granola bar and a can of soda. "That's all I found. Sorry."

The poor man didn't appear too comfortable with the way she was being treated. She smiled and accepted the food. "Thank you very much. God bless you."

The guard opened his mouth to speak, but just then, the door opened. Violet took a bite of the granola bar and popped the can of soda open. She savored the fizzy liquid as it worked its way down, cooling her parched throat. Considering how the atmosphere in the room had changed, she knew who had entered without glancing up. She ate up more of the granola bar and drank half the soda before she met his gaze.

Arms crossed over his chest, he leaned against a table, watching her. And fumed. She could see it in his eyes. He dipped his chin. "Eat. We'll chat when you're done. Perhaps, then, you might be inclined to give us what we need."

She would say, no, she wouldn't. But she needed the food. So she finished the snack, drank the remaining soda, and set the empty can on the table. "What *do* you want, Pete?"

Moving away from the table, he drew a chair, flipped it

around, and sat facing her, with the back of the chair to her. "I want what you're holding back. The ten percent. Now. No games."

"I don't have it."

"Who does?"

Silence followed.

"You've pushed me to my limit, Vi, and I'm sorry for what has to happen if you don't cooperate. You should have just done what you were paid to do and given it all over. Holding things back gets you in trouble."

Violet steeled her spine. "Handing things over places, possibly, millions of people—their privacy and probably their lives—in jeopardy. Is that a chance you're willing to take? Because I'm not."

Pete huffed. "Listen to me. There's no need to play a hero here. Simply do what you're asked."

"No. I won't." She pointed at Pete. "You should take a stand for what you know is right."

"It's not so simple."

"Yes, it is. Cancel everything. If you took anyone's money, refund it. Destroy this software before it destroys you."

"Destroy it?" Pete's brows furrowed the way they did when he'd faced a mathematical problem he hadn't yet found the answer for. "Never."

Violet sat back. "Then you're the one who made the wrong choice, not me."

Just then, one of his men entered, handed him an envelope, and whispered into his ear. Pete frowned, opened the envelope, took out something—Was it a photograph?

Before she could sneak a glimpse, he'd shoved it right into the envelope and swallowed hard. His face pale, he cleared his throat and glanced around the room.

Then his gaze settled on her. A hard edge curved his mouth, and determination glistened in his eyes. "Don't make this harder than it needs to be. I won't argue on this anymore. What you have done... Let's just say options as to what needs to be done to remove any obstructions in the way are not good. As a matter of fact, the only thing standing between you and...certain death is me. And if you continue to reject cooperation..."

They stared at each other.

But Violet was no longer scared. She wasn't moved one bit.

Her focus shifted then. She wasn't sure whether his threat did it or plain exhaustion from fighting someone who was supposed to be protecting her. Her spirit grew burdened and full of pity for her brother once more, but the worry and despondency dissipated. Trusting the Lord to fulfill His promise about Pete, at His time, she leaned forward. "I'd like to remind you of someone I once knew." She crossed her legs. "Someone I looked up to at one time. They were my guiding light, and I trusted their example."

"Violet..."

She held up a hand. "If you're going to kick me out of this

place built by our parents, Pete, give me the honor of saying my last words on these grounds."

He stared at her. And shut up.

"This person, like I'd started to say, had eyes like fire. But they burned to protect me. But not anymore. I held onto some sweet memories of our growing up over the years." She chuckled, reminiscing. "Like when you fought the boy who stole my snack money at Walmart. Or the day we walked home in a snowstorm, and Mom and Dad were stuck in Denver. You took off your winter jacket and gave it to me and walked home freezing. I never forgot that."

His Adam's apple bobbed.

"I'm not sure what happened to change you to the man you are now. But I want you to know that Jesus still loves you, is still holding out His hand of love toward you and waiting for you to come home. You have a home in heaven. Don't miss it. Don't miss *us*."

Violet sighed. "I would say more, but that's all that matters. I hope you don't hurt me, and I hope you can pause and think about what you're doing, for whom, and why. I hope you choose the right side and not the wrong side. Nevertheless, Pete, I love you, and whatever happens, I forgive you wholeheartedly. No matter what, you will make heaven."

He was silent for a while, eyes soft and brow contorted. Then the harsh glance he shot her as he rose to his feet and asked his guards to lift her up, was so different from her twin that it was almost like comparing soft bread and a rock. This Pete was cold and calculating. That left her to wonder what happened in that boarding school? Why had he returned home...heartless? She tried to find common ground with him, but each time, the ground kept shifting away.

When she thought they might've turned a corner—like at their dad's funeral when she had gleaned some of the kind-natured person he used to be—he changed and became harder and more distant.

Then a song pierced into Violet's heart with undeniable certainty and brought coolness to her mind. "Blessed Assurance" sang in her heart as Pete walked her out of the Cortexe Corp. main office building, toward the resident interns' building. It sang louder, even stanzas of the hymn she'd forgotten played back in her soul word for word. She felt her spirit gravitate toward the song, and her heart grew calm. Conflict surrounded her, but inside she had peace. She couldn't call the cops now, even if she wanted to. She couldn't change Pete's mind either.

When they walked outside, it was dark and quiet, likely the wee hours of the morning. Darkness covered the horizon, meaning most people were asleep. Where was Mike? What was he doing at this hour? His phone had entered voicemail when she'd called this afternoon. He'd mentioned that, if he was sanctioned off the grid in preparation to take down The New Rulebook software, then he would be unreachable. She should have left a message for him.

Something to tell him that she loved him, that she appreciated him, that she would miss him. But if she did so, he would ask questions—questions she couldn't yet answer.

And she didn't want to see his heart broken. If Mike had even the slightest hint that she was in danger, at the hands of her brother, he would storm the Cortexe Corp. grounds—and he might get killed by Pete. She couldn't risk it. Tim was already in a coma because of her. She wasn't sending anyone else into danger. She would face this cross alone.

"Blessed Assurance" continued playing in her mind, even as Pete walked her up to a certain room and his guards forced the door opened.

They stood and observed as Pete questioned a young lady. Only when Violet was brought in full view with her did she recognize the lady. She'd asked her the previous day to place the journal in her car to assure its safety from Pete in case he searched her office.

Pete threatened the intern. But as he spoke, "Blessed Assurance" sang louder in her mind—almost as though the lyrics became physical and imprinted themselves on her heart.

A new sensation took over her...as though her body was still here on earth but her spirit was fully with God in heaven. The sounds she was hearing were new and unheard before—angels singing praises to the name of Jesus, a choir chorusing praises to God in unison, and her spirit sang "Blessed Assurance" to Him. And it felt as if she was singing it face to face to her Savior. The room got more chaotic, but Violet found it harder to focus on Pete's threats. His voice dimmed in to the background, and the song soared above it.

Finally, tired of witnessing his continuous barraging of the young lady, she said, "Listen to me, Pete. She's done nothing wrong. Leave her." She wasn't sure of her exact words, but they seemed to have riled Pete even worse. He seized her hand, said something cruel she couldn't hear above the voice of the heavenly choir, and handed her off to his guards.

They took her and led her out of the building. The minute they stepped outside, in the darkness of night, flashes of light began to work into her vision. She began to pray in the spirit, with her whole heart, and her whole body trembled as the words came out. "Father God, as long as I'm still in the flesh, I still have the right for intercession. Therefore, I plead with You, dear Heavenly Father once more. Save my brother. Save Pete, according to Your divine promise to me. I know You promised already, but I'm praying for there to be a performance of that which You have spoken. As You promised to me, dear Lord, please do."

They sat her down inside an SUV until dawn, and she dozed off a few times. The men made flurries of phone calls outside her earshot.

She prayed on and on until they strapped her in and drove to an unrecognized location—an abandoned building next to the road. It seemed as though her car had been towed to the location. They stopped behind it. She glanced around, but maybe because it was quite early in the morning, the street was deserted. "Take this package." They shoved something into her hand, and the envelope crinkled, but she didn't look at it. "We will drive you to this address, and someone will meet you there. One of our men will drive with you. But you will be in the front seat. Understood?"

She was too tired to argue. Everywhere hurt. Badly. "'Blessed Assurance, Jesus is mine. O what a foretaste of glory divine,'" she mumbled. Then she smiled, still hoping, searching for a possible means of escape. A weird sense of peace overrode any fear she might have had.

She felt herself get shoved into the car and buckled in. One guard drove, while another held a gun to her back. The man came to a speed hump too fast. The car jolted, thrusting her forward, and something drew her attention.

Desperate to try anything to help her escape, Violet startled. The jolt had dislodged the glove box improperly shut by the intern. Her journal tumbled out, the hard corner cutting into the top of her foot exposed in her pumps. She bent over, acted like she was coughing loudly, slid it under her jacket, and pinned it to her body with an arm.

Soon, the car parked when they arrived at a construction site at sunrise. "Get out. Go and deliver this package. Someone will be there to accept it from you." They drove her all this way to the middle of nowhere only to deliver a package? That couldn't be true. But their voice drew her back to the present. "Remember, we are watching you."

She accepted the flat envelope with her free hand and walked forward. She made a few turns and glanced back— could they still see her? Only the taillight of the car was clear. So, she surveyed the area. Maybe she could go ahead to make the delivery, then make a run for it?

As she neared the place, Violet chose to abandon their delivery. She shoved their package underneath a cement block and moved forward. If anything was getting shipped, it would be her journal, with the destructive secret hidden inside it. Because, God willing, she would either destroy that software and protect the world or die trying. But, if she mailed the journal, wouldn't it end back up in Pete's hands? She bit her lip and prayed.

26

"Then we who are alive and remain shall be caught up together with them in the clouds to meet the Lord in the air. And thus we shall always be with the Lord." -1 Thessalonians 4:17

Violet walked toward the main construction site. She had to find a place to hide her journal if mailing it was not an option. But she was already at the pickup destination and couldn't turn without attracting the attention of whoever was watching.

She approached the unfinished building and slowed, surprised to see somebody was already standing there, probably waiting for the delivery. The young lady appeared businesslike in her sleek leather jacket with her dark but straightened hair waving against the wind. Square shoulders that seemed able to bear more responsibility than that of a simple delivery stood as a contrast against the uncompleted building behind her. Was that resoluteness behind those warm brown eyes? Her dark skin glowed, and sincerity shone in wide eyes beneath full lashes needing no mascara.

If Pete sent this lady here to get her killed, the lady didn't fit the bill. She was too polished. Wasn't she? Violet observed the lady again and came to the same conclusion. Something was off.

But her brother could only have forced her to a place like this for one reason—to take her out. Shivering, she made up her mind to forgive Pete for whatever he might have arranged against her. Kicking her out of the company was the worst she'd thought he would do. But this...

She remained focused and refused to take offense. Now, she understood why God warned her. If she died holding a grudge against her brother, she would miss heaven. The vision had given her time—time to be angry, time to forgive Pete face to face, and time to prepare her heart for eternity—if things went that far. It was no use holding a grudge when she knew God was in control, even now. But Violet still hoped for a chance to escape, a chance to still live here, a chance to escape Pete's plans.

As she settled her gaze on the lady, and their eyes met, a bright light shone ahead. She thought it was a reflection of the daylight and the sunshine—but the sun shone from behind, not ahead, where the light originated. Then a chorus of singing voices followed. Then she heard the voice of the Lord instructing her, His voice even clearer now that it had been at the church. "Give her your journal, Violet."

Violet scanned the lady, unsure that she could trust her. "Why don't you shoot me first?"

But the chorus grew louder and louder. The voices were so beautiful that Violet was tempted to join them. The lady stared at her like she didn't understand. So, she wasn't the killer?

"Give her the journal. Now," the Lord instructed, His voice clearer once more.

So, Violet faced the lady fully. "They can see everything. Nothing is hidden from it." The lady frowned, scrunching her smooth forehead, and said something. But Violet could barely hear her. With the urge in her spirit, Violet hurried to complete her statement. "It's called The New Rulebook. They can see everything." She handed her journal over—her most precious possession, besides the locket bequeathed by her parents which she'd left at Tim's bedside so he could see it when he woke—in obedience to the Lord.

By now, the chorus was so loud.... Could the lady truly not hear them? The journal left her hands as the lady accepted it. A figure appeared before her, glowing in white, beyond the lady. He extended her a hand, and Violet blinked against the light surrounding her.

The chorus sang louder—deafening, but beautiful

refrains. Having heard their song over and again, Violet could sing the lyrics now. She'd never heard words sung so beautifully anywhere. She reached out, accepted the hand of the figure that looked like an angel.

As soon as her hand melted into His, Violet felt swept off her feet by the power of the Holy Spirit. Every fiber of her being was hit with light shining from within. She could hardly describe it. The power of God permeated her pores, and she blinked again as more beings appeared, standing and bowing before the One holding her hand. That was when she realized—it was the Lord Jesus.

She heard a gasp, like it was from the lady she'd handed her journal, and tried to see, but the Lord held her hand. And her gaze. "Don't look down, Violet. Keep your eyes on Me."

So, she did. The glory she was seeing, the power she was swimming in, and the beauty she was surrounded in, were incomparable to anything she could set her gaze upon.

Her purse clattered to the ground, but she kept her eyes trained on the Lord. She was transitioning to glory—incomparable incorruptible glory.

Then the Lord reached out, and a golden crown appeared. He set the golden crown on her head and smiled. "Welcome home, My daughter. You served your Lord faithfully. Now, enter into His rest."

A slight pause followed. She scarcely resisted shutting

her eyes, sure the intensity of light and glory before her was more than she could take. Glory upon glory showered over her.

"Violet," He, with fire-like light for eyes, looked at her, laying her soul bare before Him. "I heard your final whisper, your final intercession for your brother. Yes, Pete shall be saved," the Lord said, and his assurance bore the signature of certainty.

She knew it would be done, according to His Word.

Violet shut her eyes as The Lord settled the golden crown on her head. She had indeed left the earth, but she didn't ask Him how. She was here, with Him, for all eternity. And the Lord would keep His promise to her, and indeed Pete shall be saved. "Thank You," she whispered.

JOHN HAD JUST ARRIVED AT THE CONSTRUCTION SITE WHERE HE worked when he found one of the vents reported as blocked. "It's too early for this," he muttered as he walked toward the building. He'd thought they'd finished on this site, but apparently, something happened at the last minute. "Like it always does."

He beckoned one of the nearest workers, who had just arrived, to him. "Hey, Carlos, can you come with me? We need to climb high-rise Number 1 to take a look."

"Sure. Let me get my stuff." Carlos grabbed his tools.

John strode ahead of him, and he was grateful the elevators here were being fixed but were still up and running. Taking the stairs for the first half of the building last week had been rough.

When they reached the floor with the vent out, he sent Carlos to check it out. Trying to hurry the process, John traced the route of the air vent to see where the air stopped flowing. Maybe, if a piece of protective nylon was sucked in, he could take it out and be done with it.

The door to one of the completed offices was partly closed. But he'd instructed the site manager to have the men leave the doors open for easy perusal.

Frowning, he approached it, then froze. A man in black stood at a window with his back turned—and a rifle in his hand. John sucked in his breath and ducked behind a concrete wall. He held his breath and wished he had a way to warn Carlos, working in the room at the other end. John shuddered when the rifle fired a shot. He winced at the sound, hoping it didn't hit anyone.

He dashed back to the other end and warned Carlos about the shooter and led him to hide. While Carlos hid, John returned to the door. A second person with a gun ducked. There were two shooters after one person? His heart pounded in his chest. Then he prayed as Angel and Tim had taught him. He slid back fully inside the room, hid, and hoped he and Carlos would make it out alive.

Soon, hurried footsteps followed the shot, leading away

from the floor where they were, and he exhaled. Whoever they were, they were leaving. But he had to protect both himself and Carlos. So they waited an additional half hour before venturing out. They glanced around, came out, and went down the building using the stairs.

As soon as their feet hit the first floor, he called the others, who hadn't come in to work yet, and dismissed his men for the day, then hurried to his truck. He thought about calling the police but stopped. Considering his past wrongful choices, if something bad happened, they would look at him as a suspect. He could only trust his sister to believe him. Thankfully, she was a cop and reaching her and explaining things to her was only a half hour drive away. He drove straight to the SSPD, intent upon telling his sister what he saw.

When he arrived at the SSPD, he turned off his truck and paused for a moment, sitting in the parking lot, wondering if he'd witnessed a murder. After all, he didn't see a victim, didn't hear a scream, and wasn't sure what he saw had meant. Maybe he'd made a mistake in coming here. He should've checked out the scene first to see if someone did get shot before rushing here. But he'd been too shocked and had only thought to protect his other employees. He confirmed with their office that his men were accounted for by the time he left and had all driven off in their vehicles.

But what if someone had been hurt? He shook his head and made up his mind. He would tell Angel what he'd seen.

Then he'd leave it to her and the cops. At least, he had cleared the building before leaving the site. As he opened his door and swung one leg out, something hit him hard on the head. He tried to turn, but another blow landed on his back and a third hit his head. There was no time to fight back. He blacked out.

ANGEL PEERED AT THE TIME ON THE WALL OF THE SSPD AND wondered why the morning felt long. She had had a restful couple of days since closing the murder case and couldn't have felt more accomplished. The grandma was in jail, and her surviving grandson was held for questioning. Apparently, this wasn't the first time they'd gotten their hands dirty. So many things were getting uncovered from their activities in the past twenty years. Some were too much for her ears to handle, so she simply moved on to her next case while another detective wrapped things up.

She checked the time. Too bad, she couldn't visit Tim at the hospital at lunchtime. She and Violet had alternated their schedules. She watched Tim for an hour over lunch, and Violet took the evening shift while Angel was busy. It worked well, and she was getting to know Violet better. Which made her wonder why Tim and Violet never became an item. She was glad Tim chose her, and apparently, judging from what officers had recovered from his pocket before he was wheeled unconscious into surgery, he had bought an engagement ring and would've proposed. Her chest tightening, she prayed she and Tim wouldn't lose their chance at love. She couldn't bear the thought of losing him, so she avoided such thoughts.

Angel walked over to the coffee machine, made a cup of coffee, and added some sugar and milk. She was walking back to her desk when Pierce drew to a stop. "Oh, I see John is here. Where is he?" He looked toward her office.

She frowned. "No, he's not."

"Yes, he is." He pointed outside. "His truck's outside. And he must be in a hurry to have left his driver's door open. Tell him I shut it for him."

Angel blinked. "Pierce, John is not here."

They glanced at each other.

"And he never leaves his truck door open." The cup slipped off her hands and hit the ground with a thud. The hot fluid poured over her boots, but she didn't care. Pierce ran ahead outside. As soon as they emerged, she could hardly breathe. Not out of a health situation, but out of fear for her brother.

They reached the truck, and with the hook of her cuffs, she pulled the unlocked door open. It swung to a standstill, and she surveyed the sight. "His bag is in the front passenger seat. The truck is still warm, so he was in here not too long ago. The key is in the ignition."

Something was wrong. She shivered.

"I'm going to get the captain," her partner said.

"Your keys, please." Her cruiser's keys were sitting on her desk, and she wouldn't waste time to go inside to get them.

"Here." He tossed his to her while running back inside, and she caught them.

Swinging around, she ran toward his cruiser. She dialed John's number, but it went straight to voicemail. Frustrated, she searched for the right key in the bundle. If someone had taken John, she hoped they were still close by. "Lord, please keep John alive. Please, Lord." She recalled the threat of the grandma sitting in jail. Were the woman's gang in-laws after her brother as punishment? Angel shoved the thought away and focused. John needed her, and she would not fail him.

Reaching Pierce's cruiser, she yanked the door and slid inside. It was cooler than John's, having had no human occupant for a few hours, so she rubbed her hands together to warm them up before sliding the keys into the ignition. She revved the engine and drove off the parking lot. She entered the traffic, lost as to where to go or where to search. So she started with the last place she knew he had been in contact with as they left home. She called his job with the number he had given her.

"Hello?" she said as soon as someone picked up. She scanned the streets, driving slowly and searching for signs of unusual activity.

"Hi. Thank you for calling Happy Home Builders Inc. How may I help you?"

Angel swerved to avoid a car that got too close, or maybe she got too close to them. She wasn't sure. "Yes, I'm Officer Angel Martinez. I'm trying to locate my brother, John. He works with your company."

"Oh, right, John. He dismissed his guys for the day and told one of them he was going to see his sister who is a cop. I'm guessing that's you."

"Yes, that's me." This wasn't good. "He got to the station, but no one has seen him. Do you know why he sent his men home?"

"One of the guys, Carlos, said John heard a gunshot on site, and they hid until the shooter was gone. So, he sent everyone home. Carlos didn't call the police because John was going there. Moreover, he said he saw nothing. But we have called the police to report the incident, and we were waiting to hear back from John. We had left him a voicemail as canceling the day's work is not our documented procedure."

And John likely knew that. So why did he choose to dismiss the workers, send them home without calling the cops, and then disappear in her parking lot?

Angel groaned inside. "What's the address for the construction site where this happened, please?"

They dictated the address, so she parked by the street and punched it into her navigating device. "Thank you." Driving as fast as she could, she called the station and updated them through the radio.

"I'm sending you backup now. And Pierce is coming with," the captain informed. "Please be careful."

"I will."

Angel called her siblings next, asking if any of them had heard from John. Their replies only worsened her worry. At the construction site, she surveyed the area from inside the car while waiting for backup. Calm surrounded the street, and nothing appeared out of place. Of course, she hadn't walked farther inward, but the captain would be incensed had she hopped out of the cruiser and headed to a possibly dangerous crime scene without backup.

Secondly, she knew her brother. John would not call his men to go home without a reason. Something scared him, and he didn't scare easy. To find where John had gone to or disappeared to, she needed to see proof of whether something happened here. Whatever scared him was here. Somewhere.

The wail of police sirens got her jumping out her cruiser, ready to go. She stepped down as Pierce emerged from a cruiser parked behind hers and walked over to meet up with her.

"Ready?" He had his weapon drawn, head lowered.

She drew hers as well and gave a nod. She led the way as they lowered their heads, trailed by other officers. Treading over leftover construction equipment and broken glass, pounding over concrete dust, and watching for the signal from the officers climbing the high-rise to provide cover, she turned a corner near an unfinished building. She saw a lady's feet on the ground peeking from the distance, and even before she saw the full form, she knew they were in for a long day. Did John see something happen here? Did it spook him?

She sighed and wished this new matter didn't hit this close to home. She swallowed harder, and as they came up on the body, she gasped and her knees buckled.

"No!" Not Tim's best friend, her friend, Violet. She spun, her eyes met Pierce's, and she passed out.

27

"And whoever compels you to go one mile, go with him two." –Matthew 5:41

Tim tugged his eyes open. The first thing he saw was Violet's golden locket, the gift from her parents, where it hung off the foot of a bed he lay in. A smile stretched his cracked lips, and it hurt. Then he looked around. He was in a hospital. He felt as though he'd just woken up from a long sleep—but how long was he out? And why?

But he was not alone. A nurse in the room was busy attending to his IV. When she saw that he had woken up, she ran off and called the doctor.

"He's awake! He has woken out of his coma," she rang out as she disappeared through the door.

Coma? Tim frowned. He hadn't felt like someone in a coma, just like he'd slept for a long time and was ready to wake up. But he had more than that on his mind. He had to see Violet and tell her about his strange dream—a dream about her.

Soon, a doctor entered the room, interrupted his thoughts, and checked his vitals. "What is your name?"

Tim remembered his name and address. But not what happened in the past year. The doctor asked about the last place he was and how he ended up in the hospital, but he couldn't recall.

"Don't allow that to bother you. Temporary amnesia is common when patients wake up from comas," the doctor assured him. "Give it time. It will all come to you."

They soon left him to rest before another interview to assess his mental state. Judging from the rawness he was feeling, he might not be leaving the hospital for a while.

Tim managed to lean up from his lying position for a sip of water the nurse had brought. Waking up from a coma, having missed so much news from the people he loved, was tough enough. But his experience just before he woke puzzled him more.

He'd seen Violet, but she looked different—radiant, standing at a beautiful distant gate. She smiled, and she glowed in light. He wanted to talk to her, ask her how she was in that place, where they were, and why she glowed and he didn't. But she'd swept past him to go inside, leaving him now at the gate.

Then he opened his eyes.

Had it just been a dream? He hoped so because it had felt so real. Once they completed his next medical check, he'd ask the nurse to help bring the hospital room's phone closer.

He had to call Violet and tell her what she saw. He had to hear her voice. Feeling like he was forgetting something or someone, he tried as hard as he could, but he couldn't recall what. He lay back down but didn't want to sleep again, in case he didn't wake up. The doctor had confirmed he'd been in a coma before a flurry of medical staff poked and prodded to their content.

While he contemplated, a nurse entered with a wary look.

He smiled at her. "You thought I'd be asleep again?" He shook his head. "Not for a while."

At his comment, she smiled back. "That crossed my mind. Are you comfortable? Do you need something to eat? You should be hungry."

He was, actually. But his thoughts were so busy he'd forgotten to ask for food. "Sure. I could use some food."

As she walked toward the door, she paused. "Oh, your girlfriend said to call her as soon as you wake. I'll call her shortly."

Tim frowned. His *girlfriend*? He had a girlfriend? He

cleared his throat. "Do you mean Violet?" Maybe she'd finally come around to seeing him as more than a friend.

The nurse's platinum bob bounced as she shook her head. "No, she's not Violet. I don't think so." She blinked. "Oh, your memory."

"Right." He nodded. "I can't remember recent history, so if I have a girlfriend, please tell me about her before she gets here. I'd not like to shock her as soon as she walks in."

She smiled and reentered. Her glance trailed his to the locket. "I see someone left you a good luck piece."

"Would you mind handing it to me, please?" he asked and she obliged. "Thanks."

She perched on a chair and glanced at the door. "I have to make my other rounds, but for a man who just came back to the land of the living, I can spare a few minutes." She raised a finger. "Oh, give me a second." She dashed out of the room.

What had been so urgent?

Tim held Violet's locket. Reading the sticky note taped to it, and recognizing her handwriting, he grinned. *To my favorite digger, I left this so you'll know I came. See you when you wake soon. Cheers, Vi.*

Of course, she would leave something valuable of hers with him because she knew he understood how important the locket was to her.

The nurse returned, clutching something. She sat back down, and excitement glistened in her eyes. "Your girlfriend is a cop."

"A cop?" Tim swallowed past a tight throat. "How did I get comfortable enough to ask a *cop* out?"

She laughed but still hid what was in her hand. More curious, he raised himself up on one elbow to meet her eye to eye, but she just shook her head. "Well, you'll need to ask her when she gets here. But she's really nice."

"What does she look like? Do I have a cellphone?" Maybe he could see her picture on his phone.

Touching his arm, she drew his attention. "There's something important you should know in case someone already called her and she's on her way here." She placed a solid object into his hand. "She's seen this already, and she knows what is inside. You'll have to explain how you don't remember, but I'm sure she will understand."

Tim sat up as much as he could. He opened his palm and stared at the box in his hand. "Does this mean what I think it means?" When she didn't answer, he unclasped the box. And with trembling fingers removed the ring. A name—*her* name, Angel—was engraved inside it, and he choked with emotion. He not only had a girlfriend, but he was going to propose— and *she* knew about it—and *he* didn't remember a day of their relationship. Tim eased the ring back, closed the box, and settled it under his pillow.

"She's got a great smile." The nurse described her, not seeing his turmoil. He refused to think of how his girlfriend —Angel, according to the ring's inscription—would react if she knew he didn't remember her. Would it end their relationship for good? Or at best, make things awkward since one had these memories and the other didn't? Her name must be a coincidence. He knew only one Angel, also a cop and good Christian. But she was his friend, not his girlfriend.

Midway through the nurse's description, the door flung open, and someone entered. The nurse's description matched the face of the person standing before him—but not the condition of her appearance.

"Angel?" he whispered, too shocked to say more. So, she was his girlfriend. Realization dawned amid confusion. He grasped to remember something—*anything*. But failed.

Dust clung to her police uniform. Tears matted her hair to the side of her face, a face reddened and puffy, almost obscuring her coffee-brown eyes. Angel may not look like a girlfriend this minute, but she was his friend, and she needed a hug. He reached out both arms, and her lips trembled as she took slow steps toward him. When she reached his bed, she crashed into his arms, and sobs racked her body.

What broke her down? But from the lady he had known her to be for many years—strong and protective of her siblings and society—he'd never seen anything break her down. His heart broke for whatever caused her such pain. He offered her the only thing he had—comfort. "Shhh. Let it all out. You're going to be all right."

When her sobs quieted, she raised her eyes and peered into his. Long dark lashes blinked at him—how beautiful those eyes were! But that thought quickly melted with her next words. "They took John." Her lips quivered. "They took my brother." She burrowed her head into his chest and wept again, and he knew now what could break her—anything happening to any one of her siblings.

But he didn't understand, and he didn't want to rattle her by sharing news of his memory loss. "What do you mean? Who took John? Who are they?"

"The people who kill—" She grew silent, and the nurse tapped her shoulder and motioned toward the door.

"Can I chat with you outside for a moment?" The nurse led the way.

Angel nodded, straightened, and followed her out.

When they returned moments later, Angel had changed. Stiff shoulders set above her straight spine, nothing like the trusting person who'd wept on him minutes earlier. Her gaze observed him as she stopped at the foot of the bed. "They say you don't remember anything from the past year?" It came out partially like a question and like a statement. "You don't remember....me as your girlfriend? Or us?"

"Yes." Somehow, he kept his voice calm. This was hard, harder than he'd thought it would be. He'd hoped to find time to collect his thoughts and try to remember before she arrived.

Her gaze faltered. "I'm sorry, then, for assuming that you knew. I was caught up in my grief and also in the joy of seeing you awake. I'm truly sorry if I embarrassed you."

"That we were in a relationship? You have no reason to

apologize. The fact that I don't remember now doesn't mean I won't ever remember." He pointed to the chair. "Please, sit. And let's talk. I really have to speak to Violet about something. I can provide you with her number if you have a phone. It's urgent, please."

She blinked those eyes at him again. Tears pooled in their brown depths again. Clenching her fists, she looked away. "I'm sorry."

He smiled, growing a bit impatient. "It's okay. We're going to chat about what happened to your brother. But, please, dial Violet. It won't take but a minute. I promise."

"This is too much."

Tim wasn't sure what she was referring to, but the nurse was nodding and crying too. What was going on?

She backed toward the door, shaking her head. "Listen, I'm glad you're awake, Tim. But I'm sorry, I need some time, and I have to go now. I'll try to be back tonight. Please don't sleep for too long again." She dashed out of the room like she was being chased, leaving Tim stunned and the nurse trailing her.

28

"REJOICE WITH THOSE WHO REJOICE, AND WEEP WITH THOSE WHO weep."—Romans 12:15

∽

TIM ROTATED THE ENGAGEMENT RING LOOSELY LOOPED ON HIS pinky finger and stared at the ceiling. Then he tapped his thumb on the bed alongside the seconds ticking by on the wall clock. It had been hours since Angel dashed out, leaving him confused and with his thoughts. So, he'd asked a nurse for a phone, then dialed Violet's number. It said the phone was switched off. The voicemail was full too so he couldn't leave a message. He called her office at Cortexe Corp., and it had been disconnected. He didn't see his cellphone anywhere in the room, so he'd have to find another way of contacting her later.

Why was everyone acting weird? He looped Violet's locket over his neck and forced his taut muscles to relax. Things were fine. All he had to do was breathe. Wherever his best friend was, she knew he was in the hospital. Surely, twenty-four hours would not pass before she got in touch with the medical team. Then he would talk to her.

An hour later, they served him a light soup with toasted bread and salad, and he'd eaten it gladly, feeling like he'd never eaten food before.

Full, he felt drowsy, but he fought sleep, determined to wait up for Angel. He prayed, read the Bible someone had left beside his pillow, and listened to the news. Then he flicked through several channels, finding nothing he liked to watch. He flicked through more stations, scrolled past reality shows, and soon, he landed on a local news channel displaying information about an art show in town during a commercial break.

It would be nice to take Violet there if she wasn't busy. He checked the date it was supposed to start. Since it was happening within a few days, he suspected his doctors might not clear him to leave by then yet. He was to be under observation for some time, especially since he was still suffering what they hoped to be short-term amnesia.

He was about to turn off the TV when BREAKING NEWS flashed on the screen. He blinked at the image, wondering why it was familiar. Then recognition hit, and the newscaster's words registered. "This victim was found murdered at a construction site. Suspects are currently being pursued by police, and we will bring you updates as we receive them. Anyone with information about this case should contact..."

The remote fell to the floor, and Tim's heart broke into uncountable pieces. "Vi?" His lips uttered her name, but he felt distant and far removed from the sound. He scrambled to reach the phone to dial the police to find out what happened, but the pain that hit his side kept him on the bed. No. Violet couldn't be dead. She couldn't have been murdered. He pounded his fist on the pillow. "Nooooo!" Pain swept over him and unleashed a storm of emotion.

He bowed himself over the bed and wept. The puzzle pieces began to fall into place. This was why Angel fled. She didn't want to break the news to him.

His best friend was gone forever. Who killed her? And why? He raised his eyes to the TV and wished the news away. Then he recalled his dream.

So, what he'd seen was real. Violet was dead and had gone to be with the Lord.

He grasped a fistful of the bedsheet. How was he supposed to live without his best friend to whom he never said goodbye?

Tim cried until he grew limp and couldn't shed a single tear. Just when he thought his heart couldn't take any more pain, the door opened. "Why didn't you tell me, Angel?" he spoke without looking. "You shouldn't have kept it from me. If you were in a relationship with me, you must know Violet and I were close."

A gentle tap on his shoulder had him looking up. A police officer looked at him with concern lining his brow. He rubbed the side of his head, leaving a peppering of gray hair standing askew. "I'm sorry for your loss. But I'm not Angel. And I have some sad news."

"I heard about Violet's death."

The man shook his head, and compassion clouded his gaze. He glanced at the TV. "We withheld the news, waiting for at least a day to break it to you. The nurse must have forgotten to remove the remote as instructed. You weren't supposed to find out like this, and for that I'm sorry."

Tim nodded, wiped his eyes, and sat up a little, his body struggling to accept his comments while his heart lay broken. "My memory loss isn't helping things either."

The man glanced at another officer who had just entered and whispered something in his ear. The elderly man frowned, then shifted his glance to Tim.

"What's wrong?" Tim held his breath.

The man was silent.

"Listen, you already kept Violet's death from me, and I had to find out in the most shocking way. Please, if something else happened, please tell me. I'm tired of getting shocked."

The man swallowed. "Angel was kidnapped on her way

here an hour ago. The officer assigned to watch her house reported it when she left her house but didn't make it here as expected."

Tim twisted the sheets so tightly it ripped. He darted his gaze between the man and his colleague, searching for the hint of a joke. But he found none. "No. This isn't happening," he flatly said, then gulped. "I must still be in a coma. Wake me up when it's over." He slid down the bed, clenched the ring box, turned his cheek on the bed, and shut his eyes. There had to be a way out of this bad dream.

A tap on his arm had him turning around. He scowled at the cop. "I said wake me up when this dream is over! Vi is not dead. John and Angel are not missing."

"Listen to me, please."

But Tim was done hearing about one bit of bad news after another. Was he back here to find out he had two people he loved and then lost them at the same time? He uncurled himself, grief overwhelming him. He glanced up with tears looming in his eyes. "Am I the reason they're dead and missing? Was there something I did wrong? Please let me die in their place."

The man squeezed his shoulder. "None of this was your fault. We can find her."

His ears perked.

"We need your help to save Angel. Before it's too late."

Tim wiped his eyes and managed to sit up. "I'm ready. Please tell me how I can help."

"We installed a device on the shoulder of her uniform due to a case she just completed where she was threatened. The device records sound and video and transmits them every twenty-four hours. Then it wipes clean and starts recording all over again. It's also equipped to transmit her location as long as it catches a whiff of some wireless signal nearby for about two minutes. We took this precautionary step hoping it wouldn't be needed but..."

Tim swallowed and tried not to imagine the pain Angel must be going through now. "What can I do?"

"The device downloads into a file, and we need you to give us the password she used so we can unlock it."

"In case you don't remember me, I'm Pierce Hollande, her partner." The other officer stepped close. "She said she'd used a passphrase you knew about should she be absent to log in. We'd created this weeks ago."

"But..." Tim swallowed. *Dear Lord, I don't remember!* "I don't even remember our relationship. This is unbelievable." *Lord, how can I be powerless when so much rests on me?*

The elderly man settled a hand on his arm. "I have just the right suggestion to help you remember. Go through your communications with her, and something will click. I believe it."

Not so confident, Tim was willing to try. "Sure." He shrugged. "I just need to find my phone."

ANGEL WINCED FROM THE ROPES BINDING HER HANDS BEFORE she sensed the cloth blindfolding her. "Argh." She tugged hard at the rope, but it didn't budge. She wriggled her body, and cold, firm steel pressed against her back. She remembered something she'd once learned, though she couldn't recall from where or whom.

There are three ways to get through a kidnapping. Confrontation, compliance, or provocation. Confront your enemy when you see an escape, comply when you don't, provoke them into a mistake and seize the opportunity.

But Angel didn't know who her kidnappers were. She hadn't seen their faces. She was barely conscious enough to see the truck had been a deep red color—nothing else. How could she allow herself to get kidnapped! She'd been so focused on getting to the hospital, seeing Tim, and asking him some questions to try to ginger his memory. She'd missed him so much it hurt, but also dreaded breaking the terrible news about Violet while she was still reeling from the discovery.

She'd also wished to apologize for her abrupt exit. Her emotions had been scattered, and she'd needed a place to pull herself together and not scare Tim back into a coma. Then a car had hit her cruiser, slamming it into oncoming traffic. Reeling, she was grabbed from a smoking vehicle, dumped into a truck, and bound by very strong hands. It happened so fast she could barely fight back, especially with the fuzziness of the accident blurring her vision. Then they knocked her out.

Now she had no idea how she got here. So, not only was her brother missing and Violet dead, she was in bondage, unable to find her brother. As it was, *she* needed to be found too. And Tim—the man she loved—saw her as no better than a friend. How much worse could her life become?

Did the SSPD know who took her or John? She wrestled her bonds once again, more worried for John than herself. He was a civilian and was not used to these situations. If she had a choice, she'd swap places for her brother. But she didn't, and worse, she'd been placed in the same situation without the swap. She practically growled her frustration.

The door squeaked open, and light warmed her face. She blinked away the harshness beneath her blindfold. Someone was there. She wanted them to speak so her recording device could pick up their voice. She hoped and prayed that the SSPD team would get the recording. "What do you want from me?"

Silence.

Something was tossed at her and landed against her hip. She groped for it, and her fingers closed in on a hard object. Next, someone untied one of her hands, then cuffed the other to a metal pole. "What do you wan—"

A hard slap left her cheek tingling. A salty taste hit her tongue, and she sucked in her breath. She probed the object in her hand—stale pizza? Then the door slammed shut.

Now in silence and surrounded by darkness, she flexed her free arm and ate the dry meal, but fear needled her spine. Whoever took her was not interested in negotiating. They were out to eliminate her. So, she prayed hard that the SSPD would find her in time—before these kidnappers killed her.

FOR THREE DAYS, TIM BARELY SLEPT. THIS TIME, IT WASN'T DUE to a coma, but due to grief. And the heartbreaking loss of those who mattered most to him.

"Tim, are you ready?" the SSPD captain asked. The man had been so polite that it calmed his worries. He'd hoped to remember something, but... nothing yet. So, they worked on his phone, searching for clues to download any file the device recorded. Someone accessed the system and hadn't seen anything show up yet. They needed the passcode for when something did enter.

Tim glanced at the intimate text messages once again. Had he truly revealed so much about himself and his past to Angel? Just scrolling through their email and text message and voicemail communication over the past several months, he found himself loving her afresh and smiling at the words he read.

That surprised him since he didn't remember their relationship. But her vulnerability toward him was born of his toward her and evidenced in every word.

The captain cleared his throat as Tim's fingers worked the cellphone. "Listen, this can't be easy for you. But you have to keep hope alive."

Tim nodded. "Of course."

"I have another bit of news."

"Oh?" Tim glanced up. "Okay."

"We've nailed the culprit behind Violet's death." The captain paused. "It was her brother, Pete."

Fury rose like a ball of fire inside Tim, and he struggled to jump down from the hospital bed. "I'll kill him!"

"Hey! Hold it, man. Tim!" The captain held him back.

But Tim would not stay still. It took three officers to get him to calm down after a few minutes. With his heart still breaking, he sobbed. "I knew he couldn't be trusted. She should've left. Why did she stay? *Whyyyy?*"

He clutched the side of the bed. Tears mingled with pain and set his heart on a vengeful path—but God stopped him —right inside his heart. He felt the rebuke of the Lord, even before he finished forming the thoughts and planning how to accomplish it. *You don't reward evil with evil, son.*

"He could've let her live. Why did he kill her?" he murmured in prayer, even as he reluctantly let go of the hate creeping up his heart. Pete would pay.

Let him go, son. Release him from your heart.

"No." Tim sobbed harder.

It was one thing for Pete to kill Violet and him not seek revenge. But forgiving him? No. That would be a very long way coming.

He lifted his gaze and met the captain's. "I want to go with you for his arrest."

But the captain, with gray-haired wisdom, seemingly saw through him and knew Tim wasn't making a clearheaded choice. "No, dear friend. You need to stay here. Get better, mourn Violet, and be ready to be reunited with Angel when we find her, because we must. I'm not sure an angry man is who she will like to see right now. You might not remember your relationship, but I saw you two together. You were perfect. And I don't want to see that ruined." The man drew close and tapped Tim's chest with a finger. "So, please, deal with the issues in here first. Then cool off and, when you're ready, be reunited with the world."

And with those words, he led his men out and left Tim with his thoughts, and with the Lord as he twirled Violet's locket he now wore over his neck on his fingers. He bit the edge of the locket, and something clicked in his mind. And he remembered. He remembered his last chat with Angel— and the passcode she'd shared—and he shouted from the room.

The door opened a fraction, and a nurse, face awash in fear, poked her head in. "Are you okay?"

He was smiling. "Please call the captain. I remember the password. Angel's password."

29

Angel was sleeping when she heard the explosion. She jerked up from sleep as voices shouted. A round of gunfire exploded, and a vehicle started. Then the hum of an engine vibrated beneath her. She was tossed to one edge of the... container?...as it drove off sharply. Then a screeching turn followed, and chaos—with voices shouting, reverberated, and *sirens* were blaring! She scrambled to her knees, powered by adrenaline. Was it a rescue? Her head throbbed, and she could scarcely focus. She was still in her uniform—

was it possible that...? She inched her bound hands to her side and exhaled the rush of hope. Nope, the only thing missing was her weapon belt, nothing else.

She cocked her head, trying to listen, to figure out what was happening. Soon, a loud pop shook the container, and the vehicle tumbled. Angel felt her belly float, then her head hit the hard floor. Another round of gunshots rang out, and everything went silent. Her head swam—*what* was going on?

Keys jingled outside. Then a door squealed open. Someone jumped inside. Their thudding boots lulled the platform on which she lay, and she shrieked.

"She's alive! Over here." Someone drew close, and a gentle hand touched her face. "I'm with the SSPD, Angel. You're going to be okay."

Those words felt foreign. She'd waited and hoped to hear them for three long and torturous days and had given up hope. Her lips began to tremble as someone cut the blindfold from her face and released her hands from the cuffs. She blinked as more men in her favorite attire—the SSPD uniform—climbed in and lifted her to her feet. Eager hands embraced her, and she sobbed into the arms of her captain.

She withdrew and searched his face. "John?" she croaked out.

The captain's brows furrowed. "No leads yet. We're still searching." He squeezed her hand. "We'll find him, Angel."

"I...wish you found...him first." She could barely speak,

having eaten only a dry piece of pizza and drank one bottle of water for three days.

"Shhh." He wrapped her under his arm. "Let's get you home. Your love is waiting for you." He stepped back, and his men carried her and set her on a Gurney as her legs could barely stand. They bore her out of an RV, into a police van. Tim...she sighed, unable to form the beloved name. She could hardly wait to see him.

AFTER HER HOSPITAL DISCHARGE FOUR DAYS LATER, ANGEL WAS sure her heart would burst as she perched by Tim's hospital bed. When he clutched her hands and buried his face in them, she caught a whiff of his pleasant aftershave. Did he have someone bring his personal items from his house? He'd had a beard on him during his coma. But she appreciated the clean shave he now sported. "I remember, sweetheart. I remember everything." He lifted his gaze to hers, shook his head, and his dark Italian curls bounced. "I'm not sure if the deep emotions I felt when I heard that Pete had killed Violet triggered it. But I remembered telling her someone was after me. Then from there, it was like a movie playing on rewind. Everything came back."

"And?" Angel had feared their next level would be a breakup if he didn't remember. This news couldn't have come at a better time.

He kissed her hair, brought out a ring, and slid it onto her ring finger. The cushion-cut, platinum, diamond-encrusted ring shone and was snug in a perfect fit. Then he smiled. "And this. It doesn't fit onto my hand so I'd rather put it where it belongs." He toyed with a loose strand of her hair near her face.

She blinked, and his hand settled on hers again.

"Sorry, that wasn't a question. Will you marry me, Angel? I want to spend the rest of my life with you." His finger grazed the ring. "And I want to join your search for John. I won't rest until he's found." His honey-brown eyes searched her face as he sucked in his lower lip.

Angel swallowed then considered his proposal for a moment. For the past four days while she recovered, her colleagues had turned over every piece of information they had, and nothing had shaken loose about where John might be. On top of that, the doctors had strongly advised four more days of rest for her before she could actively join the search. But in her heart, at this minute, she knew she would commit to spending the rest of her life with Tim. No doubt about it. And although she wished the timing was better, and that John was home, she knew how close they had been to losing this chance at love for good. She and Tim were getting a miraculous second chance, and she wouldn't waste a moment of that. So, she replied.

"Yes." She wanted to jump and dance, but she hardly felt more than a little excited with her brother still missing, but her heart firmed resolute to find John. With Tim at her side, they would be a force for good and double their search effort.

Tim kissed her cheek. "Thank you. And sorry for the unconventional proposal," he gushed. "I will do it properly soon. I'll get down on one knee, the whole nine yards.... I just wished the circumstances were different." An exhale whooshed from him, and his shoulders relaxed.

To ease his concerns, she focused on their gratitude. "Things could've been worse, honey, so we won't live in regret. You're alive and awake from your coma. I was rescued from kidnappers—alive. We can be thankful. And yes, our focus will be the search for John going forward. And I'm glad to do it with you by my side."

His gaze traveled the length of her. Then he focused on her face again. "I'm glad they didn't hurt you. I don't know what I would've done losing Violet permanently, with John missing. And then losing you too?" He shook his head. "That would have spelled the end of me."

She rested her head on his chest and felt his heart beating strong, perfectly sure that was where she belonged. "Me too. I'm just worried about John."

He ran a hand along her back. "I'm also worried, sweet-heart, but we can pray. God is in control. We search and find John—wherever he is. We're a team, so don't go off on this alone, okay?" He searched her face again, and this time, the anxious lines atop his forehead loosened.

Her heart joyed over the man who loved her afresh like

never before. "I'm not going anywhere, Tim. I'll be by your side forever."

"I love you, Angel." He kissed her hair again and curved an arm around her shoulder, pulling her close.

Her heart bloomed hearing those words she never thought his lips would utter again. "I love you too, Tim. Now, let's go and find John. And we will succeed by God's grace, however long it takes. God will keep my brother alive."

Angel rolled Violet's locket hanging down his chest and resting near her face with a hand while her mind worked. "I have ideas of how we can get started with our search in addition to what the SSPD is doing. They're capable, but this is *my* brother. And we can't rest all of our hopes on them. We will do more, beyond what I can achieve through my job."

"Amen. I agree," Tim chimed—his voice sounding healthier and stronger—the opposite of the man who'd barely clung to life on this same bed, the man she hadn't been sure would come back to her again. Hearing him speak rang like a melody so sweet she didn't want to hear it end. And she knew that if God did this miracle, He would bring John home alive. She believed it with all her heart. And she was willing to thrust her fight where her treasure was.

Tim clasped her face in his hands and smiled, shining his pure, unfeigned love through every crinkle creasing his swoon-worthy eyes into hers. "My heart and hands are ready, my love. So, let's get started."

THE END

Thank you so much for reading **WHISPER**, the full length prequel of The Pete Zendel Christian Suspense Series! Join my VIP Readers Club here- http://www.joyohagwu.com/announcements.html -to know when the next book releases, and to receive a novella for this series titled **THE SECRET HERITAGE* starting April/May 2018** for FREE ($2.99 value)

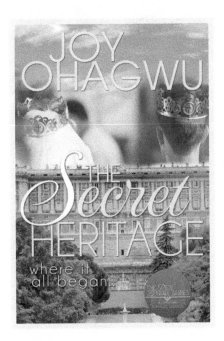

This exclusive novella reveals The Zendel family heritage dating back 100 plus years and you won't want to miss it. **Join below to make sure you receive the novella:**

http://www.joyohagwu.com/announcements.html

Please expect **HUNTER**, the next book in this series soon, by God's grace. It promises to be as exciting! God bless you!

~

A REALLY COOL OPPORTUNITY

JOIN MY VIP READERS CLUB to be the first to know when my books are discounted and available for purchase here: http://www.joyohagwu.com/announcements.html

Want to know when my next book releases?
And to grab:
* a free ebook (limited time offer)
* Release day giveaways
*Discounted prices
* And so much more!
Hit YES below and you're in!
See you on the inside!

THEN JOIN MY VIP READERS CLUB

ABOUT THE AUTHOR

By God's grace, Joy Ohagwu is an award-winning, bestselling Christian Fiction Author.

Follow her on these sites for news about instant give-aways and book updates.

FOLLOW AUTHOR JOY OHAGWU

~

You can visit and follow my Amazon Author page with one click and enjoy my other available titles.

You can also follow me on

BOOKBUB

FACEBOOK

TWITTER

God bless you!

BIBLIOGRAPHY OF MY BOOKS

~

You can visit and follow my Amazon Author page with one click. And select your next read from my available titles.

RED-The New Rulebook Series #1
SNOWY PEAKS-The New Rulebook Series #2
THE WEDDING-The New Rulebook Series #3

VANISHED-The New Rulebook Series #4
RESCUED- The New Rulebook Series #5
DELIVERED- The New Rulebook Series #6
FREEDOM- The New Rulebook Series #7
REST- The New Rulebook Series #8
SUNSHINE- The New Rulebook Series #9

BIBLIOGRAPHY OF MY BOOKS 2

UNCOMMON GROUND- Pleasant Hearts Series (Book 1)

UNBOUND HOPE- Pleasant Hearts Series (Book 2)

UNVEILED TRUTH- Pleasant Hearts Series (Book 3)
PREORDER

DECOY- Elliot-Kings Series (Book 1)

The New Rulebook Series Boxed Set- (Books 1-3)

The New Rulebook Series Boxed Set- (Books 4-6)

The New Rulebook Series Boxed Set- (Books 7-9)

Whisper- The Pete Zendel Series

Christian Inspirational Titles:

After Series (Book 1)

Jabez (After Series Novella)

After Series (Book 2)

After Series (Book 3)

DESCRIPTION

Her courageous faith defied the odds. Her heroic design saved the world from a psychopath. Now an ancient family rivalry threatens it all...

***

It was bad enough for Violet Zendel that her twin brother hated her and avoided her like a plague because of her faith. When he became the CEO of their parents' company, she did everything she could to support his success. Then she planned a vacation to help bridge the gap between them and improve their relationship.

However, when the news about a shocking event reached her ears during the trip, it shook her to her core—and led to a trail of broken hearts. Violet saw no other option but to shift her focus from pursuing corporate achievements, to preserving her family members and their legacy. But that came at a very high cost. And in the process, she is challenged by riskier choices, which demonstrate in dangerous ways, that not everything was as it seemed.

Police Officer Angel Martinez was not a stranger to hard work. She had almost single-handedly guided her four siblings into adulthood and did not feel threatened when a murder case landed on her desk. Feeling confident about her ability to solve the murder, little did she know that some cases came with decade-old secrets that could tear apart the peace and unity of those she held dear. Can she solve this case without losing her life and that of her precious family members?

Tim Santiago loved his career as an Archeologist. He seldom walked past old things without stopping to admire them, and he yearned for his best friend, Violet, to gain an appreciation for his profession. When events at a funeral unleashed a storm of mysterious phone calls and a dangerous chase, he quickly agreed that some old things were better left buried. But when he suddenly lost someone dear to him—and was close to losing two more—he faced a critical choice about unearthing more secrets. Was he already too late?

What will happen to Violet, Angel, and Tim?

WHISPER is the full length prequel of the highly anticipated **PETE ZENDEL** Christian Romantic Suspense Series.

The Pete Zendel Series is a spin-off of The New Rulebook Series—a 9-book acclaimed series. If you have not read The New Rulebook Series, start here-

ASIN- B076F5RT79

Read **WHISPER** now.

***

*This book is a spin-off of The New Rulebook Series. If you haven't read The New Rulebook Series, please do so as that will enhance your understanding of this series. Thank you!

NOTE TO THE READER

Thank you so much for getting **WHISPER**, the full length prequel of The Pete Zendel Christian Suspense Series! Although Whisper is a prequel, however, it is a full length novel.

I would like to give credit for the three lessons from Angel to John, which I paraphrased from something I heard being shared on my birthday this year (the fictional birthday, and my actual birthday was only a coincidence as I had likely written the scene much earlier). It was a young man who worked with Integrity music who was online on a livestream, and had played some worship songs on their Instagram handle on Feb 5, 2018. I was blessed by his music and message. I was writing Whisper that day, and the young man said these: "The Cross has the final Word. The name of JESUS is above that situation. God is good and in every situation I will praise Him." Those words spoke to me and I felt led by The LORD to include them in Whisper. It is the first and only time I've added any words from another person that were not expressly revealed to me by the LORD to any of my books, therefore, even though I don't know his name, I would like to give him credit regardless. Thank you.

Please expect **HUNTER**, the next book in this series soon, by God's grace. It promises to be as exciting! God bless you!

~

A REALLY COOL OPPORTUNITY

Join my VIP readers club to be the first to know as soon as my books are available for purchase here: http://www.joyohagwu.com/announcements.html

Want to know when my next book releases?
And to grab:
* a free ebook (limited time offer)
* Release day giveaways
*Discounted prices
* And so much more!
Hit YES below and you're in!
See you on the inside!

THEN JOIN MY VIP READERS CLUB

DISCLAIMER

This novel is entirely a work of fiction. As a fiction author, I have taken artistic liberty to create plausible experiences for my characters void of confirmed scenarios. Any resemblance to actual innovative developments in any scientific area is purely coincidental. My writing was thorough, and editing accurate; hence active depictions of any kind in this book are attributed to creativity for a great story. It was my pleasure sharing these stories with you! ALL glory to God.

~

Contemporary Religious & Inspirational Fiction 16. Religion & Spirituality
Inspirational Fiction

Except where otherwise stated, "Scripture taken from the New King
James Version Bible®,

All glory to God
Printed in the United States of America

❀ Created with Vellum

BOOK SAMPLE- DECOY

I

FRIDAY, JUNE 12

Rose Denison's flock of brown curls swept over her sullen face when she leaned below her medieval red dress and grabbed a fistful of wet grass while sprawled on the ground. She had to prove to herself that she wasn't dreaming. Except the moist and thick, sandy-green blades sliding between her fingers in the wee hours confirmed this was really happening. She was getting arrested—for murder.

"Ma'am. Get on your feet." A police officer with a sporty black beard flashed his badge. He stood before a background of flashing lights and a curious crowd of onlookers, some of whom she knew. He attempted to lift her off the ground, but she wouldn't bulge.

"Tomorrow is my brother's wedding day. I promised to be there," Rose protested, hoping that she was dreaming and this wasn't truly happening. That David Kings Sr. wasn't really dead. That this was all a mistake. But why then would David Kings Jr.—the only man whom she was sure truly loved her and had said so—be towering over her right now, sobbing?

Green grass, damp from rain, smeared her red, flowing, medieval party dress with a greenish, dark-brown mash as the officer gripped her elbow painfully and hauled her to her feet.

Standing, she refused to meet David's eyes as she brushed past him. She feared the heartbreak and pain etched within those ever-kind, gray-brown eyes—pain she was being blamed for causing. It could drown her. This whole mess was real. She was living a nightmare—just like her mother—but she wouldn't go back there yet, if she was to survive *this*.

She'd imagine David's hurt—rather than see it. She was mourning his dad's death, just like him, but alone. The crushing pain of the loss of a generous man who had reached out to her in kindness, offered her a job, and given her a chance—in a small town where her family's reputation was far from stellar—nearly squashed her. She'd barely returned to Elliot Town in Detroit—her hometown— seventy-two hours earlier to begin the job of a math teacher at Elliot-Kings Christian School, and she was already in trouble.

"Your hands." The officer shoved her hands behind her, twisting her arm. Her knees buckled, and she fell leftward into a brown puddle in front of black, shiny shoes dusted with clean dewy raindrops. The very shoes she almost stepped on during the dance routine at the party. She'd laughed it off then amid mirth. Knowing the wearer, she refused again to let her head rise from its hung state.

Which was worse?

That she was getting handcuffed as a murder suspect. Or that the demised victim was David's father—her new employer and founder of Elliot-Kings Christian School, the kindest man she knew? A man who practically raised her when her family still lived in Detroit and they were next-door neighbors?

No. Rose gulped. All she wished to do was to look at

David Jr. and not only tell him she didn't kill his father, but also tell him who did it—and why. She wanted to, but she couldn't. Because she could not remember any of what occurred, leading to her current predicament.

The officer's grip tightened on her elbow, but she refused to wince. She endured it, knowing David's dad had suffered a worse fate. She should be shouting her innocence at the top of her voice—except she proved nothing by doing so. Evidence speaks, and tonight, it spoke not in her favor.

She observed David's feet slide to her left, and the officer's boots stepped into view. He lifted her once again and stood her up. She couldn't help but wonder what the gathered crowd believed of her. Innocent or guilty?

She knew one fact in her gut. She wasn't a killer. She would not go down for Mr. Kings' murder while a real murderer lay loose on the prowl. No, she would not.

"Ma'am? Ma'am?" Another officer with a harried tone came around and tilted her jaw. Furious and impatient honey-brown eyes under bushy eyebrows met hers before recognition hit. Theo Sanchez, way back from grade school and close enough to be considered like family. Rose ground her teeth, shame souring her tongue. Her day just kept getting worse. Theo was her arresting officer? Unbelievable.

His eyes scanned hers. "Rose. Rose Denison? Jim's sister?" His hands dropped from her face like they'd touched hot coal. "You—a killer?" His voice took on a high-pitch tone as disbelief spread across his face and raised his brows. He excused the previous officer, led her toward a squad car, and stopped halfway, peering at her face as though trying hard to contain his shock.

Meanwhile, her heart tore into more shreds.

"Theo, you going to read the suspect her rights or do I have to?" a gruff voice asked from beneath a tree at the sidewalk where another squad car was parked on the grassy lawn. But clearly, Theo was still reeling as he posed with arm akimbo. All understandable, given that he was like extended family to Rose. He had lived with her family when his dad had died at the age of fifteen and his mom was an absentee parent. Rose was just eleven then.

He acknowledged the other officer with a simple nod but kept his attention on her. "I can't believe this," he muttered, wiped mist off his brow, and pinned her with a glare.

"Did you do this, *mi querida hermana*? Did you kill Mr. Kings?" His tone hardened as much as his face. He'd always referenced her as "my dear sister" in Spanish, his native tongue since when he lived with them, though a little older than her. This worsened Rose's anguish. She was letting everyone down notoriously just when she'd embraced obscurity.

She remained silent and looked away, unable to bear the pain flooding his eyes. "First, your mom. Now, you too?" He rushed a hand over short dark hair.

"The Rose I knew couldn't—" His voice broke, and he wiped his mouth to freeze the coming emotions.

Rose could hardly contain herself anymore. The struggle not to look at David when she was led away had taken every ounce of willpower. Now this. Her silence wasn't cutting it.

"I didn't do it," she blurted with the slight hope he might believe her. "I didn't kill David's dad. He was like a father to me."

A flash of anger colored his gaze when it whipped back to her face. "Then tell me who did." Urgency filled his tone as another officer began approaching, stepping down from the balcony behind him.

"I don't remember. I only know I left the party to go and thank David's dad for giving me a job. Next thing I know, I woke up to see David burst into an office and I was lying on the floor beside where his dad was slumped over a chair. I was scared. I honestly don't recall what happened in between."

The approaching officer with a firm hand on his belt appeared as angry as she was sure he truly was, now meters away.

"Why does your dress smell bleached, then? Did you get rid of evidence, Rose? That could make things worse." She returned her focus to Theo, who was clearly finding it harder to contain his thoughts. And to believe her. The evidence spoke against her once more.

"Will I go to a school party, with David, carrying *bleach*?" Rose rushed her next words. "I'm telling you, *mi querido hermano*, I've been set up. I need help to find out who did it and why. Catch the real killer, Theo. Please believe me. Because, I promise you, I did not—and would never have killed David's father."

"Why should I believe you, Rose?" Pressure filled his softened tone at her endearment, translated to mean "my dear brother".

She swallowed hard and chose her next words carefully as the officer growled in anger from behind Theo. "Because David is the only man who ever told me he loved me, at a time when no one else did and I was a mess. I would never do anything to hurt him—ever." He'd said so fifteen years ago when her family was going through so much. And, if memory served her correctly, she'd never responded to his declaration.

***

2

Three days earlier...

Rose had sworn to never, ever be here again.

But here she was. Back in Elliot Town in Detroit, the same town where she grew up and where her family had been scorned. Never mind that her brother, Jim, stayed in Detroit and managed to live a good life. But for her, some things were just harder to overcome emotionally.

She tried to focus on the reason for her return. David Kings Sr., founder of Elliot-Kings Christian School had offered her a job. And her boyfriend had dumped her—right before their engagement party—one year ago, six hundred and thirty-eight miles away in Missouri.

Rose blamed herself as she stood against the stubborn spring wind howling across the porch of her childhood home. It was all her fault for believing a man could be true to his word, or mean it when he said he loved her. She had fallen for it, simply wanting to settle down. Clearly, it was not to be. He seemed like a good guy before then. Always polite and cordial, and they never fought.

She huffed and curled her arms. That should've indicated something was wrong when unquestioningly George agreed to everything she said. Of course, David Kings Jr., son of the founder of Elliot-Kings School, whom she grew up next door to, was the total opposite. However, she wasn't here for David. And thankfully, she didn't see him when she went to the school earlier this afternoon after arriving in town this morning. Moreover, why was she comparing her ex to David?

She sighed and wondered again whether this move had been a mistake. But God had said to take the job. Otherwise, she wouldn't have done it.

Rose leaned over the front porch and shaded her eyes from the setting sun, eyeing the stubborn oak tree occupying the center of their yard. Her mom was right. They should have cut down the tree with holes in it. But Dad had insisted. "It gives a curve to the lawn. Leave it there. A good home for the birds," he'd argued. Though her mom wanted the space for a veggie garden, she'd let it stay. And home for the birds, it now was.

If her dad hadn't wallowed in grief after her mom's passing years ago, it could've remained a healthy tree as her mom had taken care of it when she was alive. But the man had used alcohol as his consolation as soon as the clock chimed five and he returned from his day job until midnight. Her brother, Jim, had left home then to go train at a special academy, in readiness to becoming a US Marshal. She was witness to their father's deteriorating behavior firsthand.

Sometimes he tried to sober up for work the following day, by drinking a concoction of different mixtures. Sometimes it worked, but other times it didn't. Until he retired to the relief of his boss who knew the dedication with which he worked when her mom had lived.

That could be why they let him stay those three last

years. Then he packed up and left. Just like that. He went backpacking in Europe—and hadn't come to home soil since. The latest Jim told her was that their father had now moved to Hawaii and, according to her brother, he was a changed man.

She hadn't seen him, but she doubted he had really changed. She wasn't sure she wanted to see him either, considering it could bring her past failures to the fore. Failures that began when they were all grieving the loss of her mom. Except hers had taken her farther away than she expected.

A mountain bluebird with chocolate-brown beaks squealed a call, perching between two hollow spaces of a nest's entrance in the oak. Its offsprings chirped noisily within. In the past, the sight would've excited her. Now, she simply wished she were somewhere else.

She sighed, carried the groceries she had bought, swept her hair back, and walked into the musky-smelling house. A sense of relief washed over her when she saw the weeds overgrowing their neighbor's lawn. So David wasn't in town. That left her and the new folks living on the other side of their bungalow, whom she hadn't met yet. David's absence eased the tension from this homecoming. That David Kings Sr. had offered her the job, with no influence from his son, was freeing. Since there had been no mention of David at the time, he was probably still off somewhere saving the world, like he'd said he'd do.

When David had joined the military, she was still reeling from the consequences of the error of her ways. She hid away in Clarksburg, the neighboring town, at a distant aunt's place until her tracks were well covered. At least, wherever he was, he'd remember her as the nice girl she was far from being. She was left with painful regrets, and her friend's overdose on meds had been her wake-up call.

Her eyes adjusted to the low lighting of a lone, sixty-watt bulb dangling in the long hallway. Considering it had taken one year after her acceptance of the offer from the Elliot-Kings school founder for her to join the school staff, she should have arrived earlier and cleaned the house. Instead, she delayed until the last minute, hoping an alternative would arise.

She strode into the living room where covered furniture awaited and swung her arms into a curl. She sent up a prayer of gratitude to God that she'd returned to her faith in Christ in recent years, following the horrific tragedy she witnessed. Dabbling into drugs and alcohol had been a mistake, but she hadn't known it then.

Still, her relationship with Christ now wasn't where it had been before she'd gone astray. She had too many scrapes and bruises in her heart to trust God fully yet. But she grew in faith one step at a time, part of which moving back to Elliot was.

But an uncomfortable fact remained. Uppermost in people's minds would be the fact that her mom had been jailed for murdering some random guy on the night he arrived in Elliot Town fifteen years ago. He had entered her CD/DVD rental store to borrow a film to watch in his hotel room. It was already closing time, her staff had gone home, and it was ten p.m. But on his plea, she had made an exception to serve him, not knowing she'd be the last person to see him alive.

She'd locked up the shop and made her way home while he headed to the bus stop. The following morning, he was found dead where she'd left him. After her speedy trial and serving enough time—with her fiercely denying the accusation all that time—DNA evidence proved her innocent. The real murderer was identified and imprisoned ten years ago.

But that ruined their family name. It destroyed her mom's faith, especially after their church virtually alienated them. And when she was released and returned home, she wasn't the same. Only their vacations in Hawaii brought real smiles to her eyes. Rose had lost her faith too then and gone in a direction she now regretted.

She didn't miss how people shook their heads when Rose cared to turn and look, regarding her as one of two unfortunate offsprings of a ruined marriage from the start. Except her brother hadn't seemed to bear the taint of their family's failure predicament. As it was, he was living the life as a US Marshal. She stayed away so he wouldn't be constantly compared to her sorry life. And now, he'd left Detroit. She was coming back to it. Back to Elliot Town. To start afresh. A fresh start in an old place was certainly not her ingenious plan.

She'd promised herself she'd never return once she left. Again, life ruined her plans. Getting dumped last year because she told George about her past mistakes wasn't her expectation. Working with him as her boss for another entire year, for money's sake, wasn't any easier. Every day, she'd simply wanted to flee as she watched him bring women to the school he principaled after hours. Seeing him guide them into his car and glide off to dates, while she was stuck as an observer, had added extra bruises to her self-esteem.

Sadly, a schoolteacher's salary wasn't exactly the kind you left town with. She became grateful the Elliot-Kings school offer had come almost immediately. It anchored her through those times when she'd cried herself to sleep, wondering where her life was headed, broke and alone.

She didn't tell the school when they'd offered her the job, that she hadn't wanted to accept it. In fact, God had led her to say yes by giving her inner peace, much against her will after she told them she needed to think. Then the week after she accepted, her school in Missouri announced they were closing due to lack of funding. Imagine her shock.

Considering that even after saying yes to Elliot-Kings, she searched for a whole year for another job, but the other schools in Park City, Missouri School district simply weren't hiring. They were fully staffed and budget was tight, they said. She continued her search across state lines, stopping only last week when it became clear she had nowhere else to go. She hadn't wanted to return to Detroit. Yet she couldn't stay in Missouri. Her savings from a teacher's salary were so small she couldn't live on it for more than one month, and only if she had nothing serious to pay for. She had already cut off her cable subscription six months earlier to save a little cash, and she didn't plan to install it here either.

She'd quickly realized that, one way or another, she was being dragged back to Detroit. Except if she'd turned down the job offer, she would've returned jobless. Realizing the choice had been made for her, she thanked God for giving her a job to anchor her financially. All she had in life now was her and Jesus. And for one, she didn't want her brother hearing she was back to Detroit, and Elliot Town specifically. The moment he heard, he'd assume something was wrong. With his wedding only a couple of days away, she wanted nothing to mess it up for him.

Back then, he'd begged her not to leave, so Jim knew how strongly she felt about Elliot. The last thing she wanted now was to ruin his perfect life with her messy one. More importantly, she didn't want to answer questions about the past to him either.

Thankfully, the area where Elliot-Kings school situated wasn't too crime ridden, but that could not be said for the rest of Detroit. She thought of her former high school classmates who lived in such places—how had they managed to combine school with the stress of their various trying situations? Granted, judging from what she saw earlier today when she'd visited the school upon arrival, things looked good.

There were better dressed students, and well behaved too. Some looked like they came from good homes, and most of them displayed good manners—greeting her with a "ma'am" and holding the door open for her—while others still clearly needed some home training, assuming they had a home.

She wasn't alien to troubled and at-risk kids. They were her focus. Having gone wild during her teenage years, and narrowly avoided long-term consequences because of it, she made it her goal to teach other kids to do better. Usually, a triggering situation lurked underneath it all. Many of those would need extra support in her class, and she was prepared to give it.

Turning around and gliding her luggage from the living room where she'd left it earlier, she wished she'd paid for an extra day of dusting. Cobwebs still hung from the windows around the back end behind the kitchen, leading out to the backyard where she and Jim played basketball when they were younger while he baked up something for her. She chuckled. He was always the cook while their mom was away.

The living room furniture remained covered, as it had been since the day she left. Thankfully, her parents had paid off the house before her mom got jailed. It hadn't cost much at the time when most people weren't living in the area yet, like it was now. Her brother moved out before her to another town in Detroit. Few miles separated both areas, but the difference in safety was clearly visible, judging from the scarcity of drug dealers here compared to where Jim lived before leaving Detroit.

She trundled past the boxed-up stuff belonging to her parents containing personal items like clothes, shoes, and such. Things they'd pulled together and planned to donate years ago to a homeless shelter down the block. They just hadn't gotten to it yet. Three years gone by.

Maybe now, she could make out time to get it done. She climbed past different plaques of their various achievements on the wall and gave credit to the cleaners for dusting them off. Three years plus of non-use had rendered the dining room table with one broken leg, and it was leaning over. The bend threatened to toss the tablecloth and the saltshaker on it to the floor.

She released the luggage and pushed a side stool against the table, making a note to take care of it. Then she went into the kitchen and placed the food items she'd bought into the fridge and freezer. Takeout would have to do for tonight. She just needed to figure out where to sleep on between the couch and her former bedroom.

She bit her lip. Her mom's room was where she'd typically slept during challenging times. It had felt so comforting. She shook off the pull to go down memory lane and left the kitchen.

Rose carefully passed the coat rack, wiping it first with her finger to test its dustiness. She blew off few flecks from her finger before hanging her coat. Then she proceeded upstairs to the bedrooms with slackened shoulders, feeling more worn than she'd expected. Her back ached, and she wished for a hot bath.

But the heat wasn't turned on yet, and she would need help with that. Or she could go to a hotel, which she could hardly afford. She had to conserve her spending until she received a first paycheck. A cold shower would have to do for now.

As she strolled into her old bedroom, the floor creaked. She flipped on the lights and sunk onto the bed with new sheets, lowering her head and slapping her eyes shut. Arms spread wide, she hoped to blink away the dreamlike reality. *Lord Jesus, why am I here? Why did You return me to Elliot?*

Continue enjoying DECOY BY CLICKING HERE

CPSIA information can be obtained
at www.ICGtesting.com
Printed in the USA
FSHW010948070519
57918FS

9 781980 363996